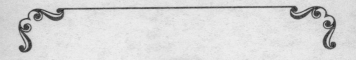

"We have no time for such silliness as reputations!"

"How fierce you are!" he said as he maneuvered her backward until he could push her down on a chair. "That is quite enough! You will sit there and be quiet, pretending to be the lady you are not. If you behave yourself, I may—mind you, I may—tell you what I am going to do."

Penny glowered at him, her full lower lip outthrust, and it was all he could do not to bend and kiss it. Wondering where such an insane urge had come from, he waited until she nodded reluctantly.

Also by Barbara Hazard
Published by Fawcett Books:

MONDAY'S CHILD
TUESDAY'S CHILD

WEDNESDAY'S CHILD

Barbara Hazard

FAWCETT CREST • NEW YORK

"Wednesday's child is full of woe . . ."

For Dee Hendrickson and
Edith Layton Felber, who are
—alas!—Wednesday's children

A Fawcett Crest Book
Published by Ballantine Books
Copyright © 1994 by BW Hazard, Ltd.

Library of Congress Catalog Card Number: 94-94040

ISBN 0-449-22209-8

Manufactured in the United States of America

First Edition: July 1994

10 9 8 7 6 5 4 3 2 1

One

England
1812

IT WAS FULL dark before an old-fashioned coach drew into the yard of the Fox and Grapes, a small wayside inn some few miles south of Stanborough. The tired team that drew the coach halted in relief before hanging their heads in the traces. Above them, the coachman slumped on his perch.

Inside the coach, seated facing back, Miss Penelope Shaw eyed her aunt Eliza shrewdly. She knew the older lady was fretting; she had planned to reach London by this evening. But the April weather had been showery, and the muddy roads had slowed them, as well as making frequent stops to rest the team imperative. Aunt Eliza did not believe in job horses.

"At last!" Miss Shaw's sister, Phillipa, sighed as she released the strap she had been clinging to. "I thought we would never reach an inn. And I cannot tell you how weary I am!"

"Poor, dear child!" Lady Eliza said, patting her hand before she collected her reticule and straightened her hat. "It has been tiring, hasn't it? Not that I can't recall a time when—"

"No doubt you can, ma'am, but perhaps we could hear of it later? I, for one, am chilled through. Just to be close to a fire will be heavenly," Penelope Shaw said in her gruff little alto.

Her sister sighed again. "Yes, to say nothing of

1

how needful I am of visiting the necessary, dear ma'am."

"Do try to preserve a modicum of delicacy, child!" her aunt scolded, although both girls noted she herself was hurrying to leave the ancient vehicle. Their groom had let down the steps, and as Lady Eliza took his arm, she gave him instructions about the baggage.

"What a very poor-looking place . . . so sinister!" Phillipa whispered as she clutched her sister's cloak and stared about. In the gloom the inn did look mean, with its low roofline and narrow windows. A run-down stable was situated over to one side, and the carts and drays that were assembled in the muddy yard did not promise a wealthy clientele.

Penelope chuckled. "Just what Aunt Eliza was looking for, of course," she whispered back. "However, it will have to serve. And I would sleep in that stable to escape another minute in our dreadful old coach. I told Aunt Eliza that the leather straps the body is suspended on were as good as gone, but you know her!

"Well, we only have a little further to go, Phil. We must pray that when we reach town, we will not have to perch gingerly on cushions for above a week."

"But even that would be worth it to be in London at last," Phillipa remarked. "Ah, Penny, London!"

In the light that streamed from the taproom windows, Penelope could see her sister's eyes grow dreamy, the little smile that played over her soft lips, and she smiled in response. For months Phillipa had been counting the days until this journey, a journey that promised at its end not only the splendors of the capital they had only heard about, but, more importantly, her come-out at last. Penelope thought it strange her sister yearned for a Season so fervently, when she was so shy and diffident in social situa-

2

tions. But Phillipa assured her that all that would be a thing of the past once she was in London.

Ever practical, Penelope was not so optimistic. She was afraid her sister would be lost there, perhaps even hurt. For if she colored up and had little to say that was not a stammer among their friends in Northumberland, why would a change of location make any difference? And in London they would be surrounded by strangers, all grand and haughty.

For herself, she did not care, although at seventeen she was of an age to come out, too, if she had wanted such a thing. But Miss Penelope Shaw had no such intention. She thought the whole thing ridiculous, and more than a little degrading, being paraded here and there to catch a noble gentleman's eye—but she would never say so, lest she destroy all her older sister's pleasure. If only she did not have the uneasy feeling that pleasure was not to be Phillipa's lot.

She pushed these worrisome thoughts of the future from her mind as they entered the inn. It was stuffy and smelled of spilled ale and cabbages cooked long ago. Loud, coarse voices and hearty laughter could be heard coming from the taproom. As Phillipa, looking distressed, edged even closer to her, Penelope wrinkled her nose in disgust.

Lady Eliza rapped her umbrella on the bare, grimy wooden floor. "Landlord, if you please!" she called out in a piercing voice. The taproom quieted for a moment, then a hum of voices began again.

A tall, thin man clutching a greasy cloth hurried into the hall, his beetled gray brows rising when he saw the ladies who were waiting.

"Sorry ter keep ye, mum," he said, thrusting the cloth behind his back as he bowed. "An' wot kin I be doin' fer ye this wet night?"

"We shall require two bedchambers, one for me and one for my nieces," Lady Eliza told him firmly.

3

Then, leaning forward and fixing him with a stern eye, she added, "I advise you not even to attempt to overcharge me for them, my good man. I am one who is not easily gulled."

The innkeeper bowed again, looking sad. "Ye've left it too late, mum," he said as he shook his head. "I've but the one room left. Custom's been brisk terday. If ye'd only come earlier, but now, well . . ."

"Only one?" Lady Eliza asked, sounding personally affronted. Then her face brightened as she said, "Well, I suppose we can make do with that. The team is done up and can go no further. You can provide a pallet?"

The landlord eyed the two girls dubiously. "Aye, but only fit fer a maidservant, I can. It won't be very comfortable fer the likes o' one o' them."

"No matter," Lady Eliza said, waving her hand. "Kindly show us to the room. The bed has been well aired? There are clean sheets?"

"Ter be sure," he said as he led the way to the stairs. "An' would ye be wantin' a private parlor and dinner, mum?"

"We will not require anything but the bedchamber," Lady Eliza told him as she followed him up the stairs. "We are weary and intend to retire immediately."

Knowing she would most surely end up on the pallet—and resenting it—made Penelope say quickly, "But surely a hot cup of tea would not be amiss, aunt? We must take care . . . lest we fall ill."

As she toiled up the flight, Lady Eliza glared at her younger niece over her shoulder. The stubborn expression she saw on the girl's face made her sigh and capitulate, lest Penelope enact them a scene, something she knew she was very capable of doing if thwarted.

"Very well," she said, her voice grudging. "Tea for the three of us then."

"That'll be a shilling apiece fer the tea an' bread an' butter, an' the room is ten shillings the night," the landlord said as he reached the top of the flight. "An' it's ter be paid in advance."

Penelope kept her face expressionless as her aunt gasped. Obviously, no matter how ladylike and refined they might appear, the innkeeper had decided they were the type who were apt to make a bolt for it on the morrow without paying their shot. But, of course, Aunt Eliza's parsimonious ways were to blame for that!

"The very idea! And ten shillings is highway robbery for such a place as this!" that lady said as she swept before him into a small room under the eaves. Its main article of furniture was a tester bed, although there was a small table and two chairs set before the fireplace. As she looked around, Lady Eliza sniffed in derision, for the room's hangings were faded and limp, and the quilt on the bed looked none too clean.

"Eight and not a penny more!" she said, sounding militant.

Before the innkeeper could begin to argue, Phillipa moaned and sank down in a chair by the fire, covering her eyes as she did so. "Please, aunt?" she murmured. "I am so very tired, and—and upset!"

Lady Eliza noted how her niece's shoulders were drooping, how her hand was trembling, and grudgingly, she nodded her agreement to the innkeeper without further ado. "Very well, but I still consider it outrageous," she said. "Now, we will need hot water, and more coal for this fire, and at once!"

When her host made no move to obey her, but only stood there stoically, she turned her back on him to fumble in her reticule for the money he was so clearly waiting to receive. As she handed it to him, she said, "I have never been so insulted! And

5

if there were anywhere else to stay this night, I would leave here at once!"

The innkeeper bowed to her, grinning now. As he turned to go, a soft voice said from behind him, "I do beg your pardon, ma'am, but I could not help overhearing your conversation as you came up the stairs. How very unfortunate you must all share a room! Do allow me to suggest that one of the young ladies come in with me. I travel alone, and the bed in my room is ample for two."

Lady Eliza stared at the newcomer, her heavy face suspicious. The woman who stood in the doorway was in her early thirties, dressed quietly in good clothes of a modest cut. She was very pretty, with an appealing smile, and she was, as Penelope was quick to note, voluptuous as well both above and below her tiny waist.

Before Lady Eliza could speak and refuse the offer, the woman went on, "But I must introduce myself so you may be easy. I am Mrs. Louisa Bellings of Manchester, on my way to London. I realize that does not tell you much about me, but as a Christian, I could not let one of these young girls spend the night on the floor. How miserable she would be! And traveling is so uncomfortable, too, even with a good night's rest, don't you agree?"

"You are certainly right about that, ma'am," Penelope said quickly. "How very kind of you! I should be delighted to accept your offer, and that way, we can all be comfortable."

"But, Penelope, I really do not think— Why, we do not even know—" Lady Eliza began, only to be interrupted by their mysterious benefactor.

"I understand exactly how you are feeling, ma'am. But I do assure you I have no ulterior motive in mind, and I am trustworthy. And may I suggest you remain in your room or hire a private parlor? The customers here are not at all genteel.

6

Far from it, in fact. If my carriage had not had a slight accident, I would never have stopped, for I fear the place attracts a very common element."

The innkeeper snorted behind her, and she turned to him. "The dinner I ordered is ready? After I have shown the young lady to my room, I shall come down at once."

As Penelope followed Mrs. Bellings down the hall, she heard her aunt begin to haggle with the innkeeper about lowering the price of the room, now that they would not require a pallet, and that man's indignant replies. She sighed. To listen to Aunt Eliza, one would have thought her only a step from the almshouse, and yet, in reality, Penelope knew it was no such thing.

"Here we are," Mrs. Bellings said as she entered a large front room and lit a candle on the dresser from the one she carried.

"Please do not look so conscious, my dear. Travel is expensive, and your aunt is perhaps only . . . frugal?"

Penelope swallowed her comment that "frugal" was hardly the word for it as she nodded and pushed back the hood of her sturdy gray cloak.

"Why, what lovely hair you have!" Mrs. Bellings exclaimed. "Such an unusual color!"

Penelope wrinkled her nose. "It is nice of you to say so, ma'am. I have always disliked it myself, wished I had blond hair like my sister, and not this blatant orange mop!"

"But it is *not* orange," Mrs. Bellings protested, a twinkle in her fine dark eyes. "It is like flame, all red and golden and glowing. And I see it is naturally curly, too. You are to be envied."

She chuckled then. "But, of course, you would disparage it. Most females dislike something about their appearance—and yearn for what others possess. A smaller waist or longer legs, a pert nose or fuller lips. I fear we are all of us capricious that way."

7

"Surely you never wished to be different, ma'am?" Penelope said, her eyes wide. "You are so lovely!"

Her benefactor swept her a mock curtsy. "But of course I did! I have always wished to be taller and slimmer, and I, like you, wanted to be fair, not raven-haired.

"Now, do you prefer a particular side of the bed, Miss . . . er . . . ?"

"Penny . . . Penelope Shaw, ma'am. And I've none at all."

"Then I shall take the far side near the window," the lady told her. "But I had best go below to my dinner. Somehow I doubt letting it cool will improve it any, not here. 'Tis a dismal place, is it not?"

Penelope tried to thank her again, but that thanks was waved away. The lady said she would order fresh towels and some hot water sent up, and indicated where the chamber pot was located behind a screen in the corner. A moment later the door closed behind her, and Penelope was left alone.

She moved closer to the cheerful fire burning in the grate and held out her hands to it. As she did so, she looked around the room, noticing the smart new portmanteau set at the foot of the bed, the scarlet cloak that hung on a peg behind the door, and the fashionable bonnet on the dresser. How lucky for her the lady was here and so kind, she thought as she went to try the bed. It creaked a little, but it seemed fairly comfortable.

After she had washed in the hot water provided by an overworked maidservant, she hung her own sensible gray cloak beside Mrs. Bellings's and went down the hall to her aunt's room. No doubt by now the tea had been delivered and their bags brought up, as well as the hamper of food that Lady Eliza had insisted on bringing with them. She claimed it was because she did not trust inn fare, but both the misses Shaw knew she did so for reasons of economy. There was only a little bread, cheese, and ham left in the basket, a few apples, and a small bottle of brandy for emergencies. Pray we reach London and Uncle William tomorrow! Penelope thought, smiling wryly. Otherwise, Aunt Eliza would be forced to spend more of her precious shillings, and how painful that would be for her!

Although she enjoyed the hot tea and the thick slice of fresh bread that was so generously buttered, she did not enjoy her aunt's harangue about her being so free with a stranger.

"After all, for all we know, the woman might be up to no good," Lady Eliza complained, frowning darkly.

Penelope saw her sister looked frightened, and she smiled at her. "But how could that be?" she asked, determined to be patient. "She is putting herself to a great deal of trouble, taking me in with her. Besides, for all she knows, I might be a restless sleeper or a snorer. I think her kind, and I am grateful."

Since her aunt continued to bemoan her impulsiveness, it was not long before Penelope bade them both good night and retreated to Mrs. Bellings's room.

She was in bed and almost asleep when that woman finally came upstairs. Through half-closed lids, she watched idly as she removed her gown and hung it up before she sat down near the fire to brush out her long dark hair. She wore only a thin lawn shift, and Penelope closed her eyes, ashamed to be spying on her. But in only a few moments, when she opened them again, it was to see Mrs. Bellings whisking the shift over her head. Wide-eyed and shocked, Penelope saw her run her hands down all her rich curves, caressing them. She swallowed. She had never seen another naked female, and she hardly ever looked at her own body, for she

9

had been taught such things were sinful. Yet here was Mrs. Bellings, who seemed such a lady, doing just that as she turned this way and that before the spotted glass that hung over the dresser.

For a moment, Penelope felt a frisson of unease and thought longingly of the hard but safe pallet she might be resting on in the other bedchamber. Perhaps Aunt Eliza had been right?

It seemed an age before her strange bedfellow lowered a white nightrobe over her nakedness, tied on a lace-trimmed cap, and came to bed. Penelope closed her eyes tightly. A moment later, she heard the bed creak as the lady climbed in and turned over on her side to face the window.

Penelope lay there stiffly as she considered such strange behavior, and she wondered if she would even be able to get to sleep. Fortunately she was so tired from traveling, she dropped off as soon as she heard Mrs. Bellings's breathing deepen.

When she woke the next morning, the room was still dark, and she knew it was very early. Beside her, Mrs. Bellings slumbered on. But Penelope was used to rising early at home, and since she was sure her aunt would be anxious to be on the road again as soon as possible, she decided she had better get up.

She edged out of bed, trying to be as quiet about it as possible, and she did not light a candle as she struggled into her warm kerseymere gown and put on her hose and shoes. Running a comb through her unruly curls and packing her night things back in her portmanteau only took a few minutes.

Suddenly she knew what she wanted to do, and her lips curved in a grin. At least she could have a brisk walk before she was cooped up in that horrid old carriage again.

In the darkened room, she fumbled for her cloak on the peg where she had hung it and let herself out, closing the door quietly behind her. She paused by her aunt's door, but heard nothing at all from within; her smile broadened. Good! They were not even up yet!

When she reached the bottom of the stairs, she saw from the light coming in through the taproom windows that she had taken Mrs. Bellings's cloak by mistake. For a moment, she considered going back for her own, and then she shrugged. She would not be gone long, and surely the lady would not mind the mistake. Besides, if she went back, she might wake her, and that would be unkind.

Safely outside the inn, Penelope took a deep breath of the fresh morning air as she pulled the hood of the cloak up over her head. It had stopped raining, and the lightening of the sky to the east promised a fine day. And, oh, how good it was to be away from the stale, fusty odors of the inn!

Reaching the road, she turned away from the village and set off at a good pace, breathing deeply as she did so. There was no one abroad, although she could hear a rooster crowing some distance away, then a dog barking in response. In an hour or so, this road might be crowded with people, carts, and drays, but for now she had it all to herself, a personal domain.

As if to mock her fantasy, she heard a carriage approach from behind and stop, and she turned slightly to see who it might be. As she watched, a groom jumped down and came toward her. Had the travelers lost their way? Well, she would be no help, for she was a stranger here.

As the servant came nearer, Penelope felt a little shiver of alarm. He was dressed in smart livery, but the grim look on his homely face startled her. Impulsively she picked up her skirts and began to run away from him. She heard his footsteps pounding after her as he gave chase, and she tried to quicken her pace. But it was no use, and only moments later, he had grabbed her by the arm to spin her around. "Not so fast, mistress," he said harshly.

"Whatever do you mean by this? Let me go at once!" Penelope gasped, as she tried to free herself. He only tightened his grip in response.

"Nay, I'll not be doin' that," he said. "Not now when I've got ye at last!"

"If—if you don't release me this instant, I'll scream!" Penelope threatened, her eyes flashing.

He didn't bother to reply, only pulled her closer in one arm while he clamped his other hand over her mouth. He was very strong, and all Penelope's efforts did her no good at all, although she continued to kick him and struggle to escape. Willy-nilly, she was borne to the coach and thrust inside.

As soon as her mysterious assailant removed his hand, she drew a deep breath to scream for help as loud as she could. That scream was cut off almost before it began by another large hand. Penelope saw that a second groom was holding her fast now, as the first one jumped inside and shut the door behind him. At once, the carriage moved forward.

Her heart was pounding so in her breast, she thought she might die from it. Who were these men? What did they want with her? She refused to dwell on any of the horrid things that occurred to her as she continued a silent, frantic struggle, kicking them with her sturdy leather walking boots and trying to bite the man who kept her silent.

"Ow! Stop that!

"We'll 'ave ter tie 'er up, gag 'er like," that groom said to his fellow. "Ow! Stop that, d'ye 'ear?"

"Aye, like a wildcat, ain't she? I've some cord 'ere. Thought it might come in 'andy. You got a clean nose cheat, Al?"

The second groom nodded as the coach, having left the village behind, careened down the rutted road at a rapid pace. Only moments later, Penelope was gagged and trussed as neatly as any Christmas goose, and the two men settled back on the squabs, one of them rubbing his shins and looking severe. Over her gag, Penelope glared back at him. She was still frightened, but now she was angry as well. How dare they abduct her? How *dare* they? Well, she vowed, she'd not go meekly to her doom, not she!

"Coo 'ee, won't the master be pleased we come up with 'er like this, an' got 'er away as neat as could be? No one saw us, neither," the first groom said, with an air of satisfaction. "Might be worth a lot ter us, Al. Ye know 'ow 'e's been frettin' since she escaped us in Grantham."

"Wonder wot she wuz doin' walkin' out alone like that?" Al asked. "She's such a wily one, from all I've 'eard tell. Seems careless, don't it?"

"Don't know. Mebbe she felt safelike in such a small, out-of-the-way village. That's why we couldn't find 'er in any o' the bigger towns with larger inns. She's been avoidin' them 'cause o' us. But we got 'er now! Can't 'ardly wait ter see the master's face when we bring 'er to 'im!"

He chortled, looking so pleased with himself that Penelope longed to hit him. Forced to be quiet now, she had listened carefully to their conversation. What master? she wondered. Who had escaped him? For it was surely not she herself, as she knew well. Then looking down at the scarlet cloak she wore, her eyes grew thoughtful. Obviously the grooms had had no intention of capturing her at all. It was all a mistake, for they had hoped to grab Mrs. Bellings! But for what reason? she wondered as the coach continued to thunder along.

And where were they taking her? The coach was headed north, back the way they had come the previous day. She hoped this master of theirs resided at no great distance. Perhaps if he did not, there

13

would be time to save herself, for when he saw she was not the woman he sought, surely he would return her to the inn.

Her heart sank then. Aunt Eliza would be all undone, and as for Phillipa, she would be sure to have hysterics as she so often did when she was distressed. And they would have no idea where she had gone, or why. Oh, dear! As frightened as she was for herself, now she was also concerned for Phillipa. All her life, Penelope had shielded her older sister, supported her through every crisis, and calmed her whenever she became excited.

As the coach continued its rapid journey to heaven knew where, she mused how strange that that must be so, when Phillipa was a full year older. But, as Aunt Eliza had been known to say times without number, Phillipa was a girl beset by nerves, and sensitive to boot. Too sensitive, Penelope had often thought, although she had dutifully stifled any criticism—no matter how often she had longed to utter it. Sometimes she had thought Aunt Eliza was part of her sister's problem. She was high-strung herself, suspicious of nature, and besides being parsimonious, far too eager to coddle her favorite niece and encourage her in her crochets.

Remembering what Aunt Eliza called her, she frowned. The groom called Al, who had not taken his eyes from her, frowned in return, but Penelope was not attending to him.

After today, she told herself wearily, "difficult" would not be the first word her aunt used to describe her, and on that she would be willing to wager anything you liked!

Two

As time passed, and the sun rose even higher, Penelope's spirits sank. So, they were going to travel some distance after all. There was no chance that she could straighten out this mistake and return to the inn in time to spare her aunt and her sister from worry, she thought gloomily.

Both grooms had dozed off, but that did her no good at all. When she had first observed their eyes getting heavy, she had tested her bonds surreptitiously and found there was no help for her there. She was well and truly tied, and until someone loosed her, she was helpless. But, she told herself, it wouldn't matter anyway, for at the speed they were traveling, throwing herself from the coach would be suicidal.

Whoever the grooms' mysterious master might be, he kept good cattle. She had never been so swiftly conveyed before. And the coach itself was nicely appointed—and so comfortable she knew it must have the new steel springs beneath it. Perhaps the man was rich? Perhaps a leader of society?

But no, that couldn't be. Society leaders did not kidnap women, not any that she had heard of anyway. Trying to picture her uncle William involved in such a nefarious scheme was not only impossible, but ludicrous. Uncle William knew his own worth too well. Starched up and proper, very aware of his superiority to the rest of the human race, he would have scorned such doings.

Penelope rested her head on the well-cushioned squab behind her and closed her eyes. There was no sense trying to memorize the way they had come, and all the turnings, for even if she were to escape, they had traveled too far from the wayside inn for her to be able to walk back. And walk she would have to, for she had not brought her reticule and didn't have so much as a penny on her person. Truly, she was at her kidnappers' mercy.

Still, and in spite of her lingering trepidation, she could feel anger growing. To think that an innocent young girl could be treated in such a way, enraged her. She would be sure to make this mysterious man pay for it, one way or the other, she told herself darkly. For she was not some little nobody, after all. She was of society herself, or she would be, once she reached London. Such indignities were not to be borne!

The morning was quite advanced when the coach slowed at last and turned in between a pair of modest gates. The drive was smooth and well cared for, but the prospect was not outstanding. Penelope was disappointed as the coach came to a halt before a very ordinary two-story house made of brick. She had rather liked her theory of a man of great wealth—who would shower her and her family with largess for so distressing her.

" 'Ere we are then, Fred!" the groom named Al said, sitting up to tidy his suit. "Will ye carry 'er in?"

" 'Ave ter. She can't walk tied up like that, I suppose. An' I'm not going ter untie 'er, that's fer sure!"

"Me neither," Al agreed hastily. "Get down then, and I'll 'and 'er out ter ye."

As she was pushed along the seat to the door, rather like an unwieldy package, Penelope began to seethe. And when Fred grabbed her around the waist and slung her over his shoulder, she was furious. Her hood fell forward over her eyes, obscuring her vision, but she felt him climb a shallow flight of steps to pound a door knocker. Well! she thought. Well!

She heard the door open, then a startled intake of breath.

"Mornin', Mr. Banks," Fred said. Penelope could hear the grin in his voice. "I got a present fer Mr. Alastair."

"The master is still in the breakfast room," a haughty voice declared. "Shall I ... er ... notify him of your arrival?"

"Ye do that, Mr. Banks. He'll be right glad ter see wot Al an' me brought 'im! Set 'im up nicely, I dessay. I'll jess take 'er ter the library."

As she was carried into another room, Penelope heard footsteps receding. Fred lowered her to her feet, but she could not see where she was. The enveloping hood still covered her face, and with the cord that secured her hands connected to the one binding her feet, she had no way to push it back. I must look a perfect fright! she thought, and that did nothing for her equanimity.

Fred was whistling softly now as he kept one hand on her arm to steady her. Or perhaps he was afraid she might suddenly break loose and escape? How ridiculous!

Long moments passed before hurried footsteps echoed in the hall beyond.

"Fred! What the devil is this Banks tells me?" a deep voice asked impatiently. There was a long pause, and then the voice said, "Oh. You *have* brought a woman here."

"Not jess any woman, guv'ner. It's the one ye've been lookin' fer! Came up with 'er early this

17

mornin' in a small village not a day's journey from Lunnon. Recognized 'er, I did, by that there cloak."

"Can it be?" the voice whispered, sounding excited now. "If it is indeed she, I'll see you profit from it, my good man!"

The groom chuckled and released Penelope. For a moment, she staggered a little, until another hand steadied her, and Fred's master said, "So, my dear, *dear* Louisa, I have you at last! And all your nefarious plans have come to naught! You should not have tried such a trick with me, you know."

Penelope was getting very tired of his gloating, and she wished he would get on with it, remove the hood, discover the grooms' mistake, and begin to make arrangements for her to be returned to the inn.

As if he had read her mind, he suddenly twitched the hood back from her face. Penelope glared at him over her gag, her eyes furious. As he stepped back, so startled his mouth fell open, she saw he was a man in his mid-twenties, of medium height and wiry build. He had carefully combed blond hair, and a rather long, thin face. With his mouth ajar, she thought he resembled nothing so much as a landed trout.

"But—but this is not Louisa Bellings!" he exclaimed. "Who is this urchin?"

"Ye mean she's not the one, sir?" Fred asked, sounding worried.

"Of course she's not!" his master snapped. "Louisa's a lovely woman with black hair, not a tiresome, untidy schoolgirl with horrid orange hair!"

"Well, but the cloak, sir! I seen it fer meself in Grantham, an' I'd swear this is the same one!"

"It might be, I don't know," the other muttered.

Penelope was so angry now, she was having trouble breathing. To think she had been lugged in here like a sack of meal, and now was being insulted as well. Untidy schoolgirl, was she? With horrid orange hair? She'd make this fop pay for that, somehow!

"Mmmmm," she managed to growl behind her gag. Her kidnappers looked startled anew, almost as if they had forgotten her.

"Yes, to be sure . . . We must untie you, take that gag off," the owner of the house muttered as he approached her.

"I'd be real careful o' doin' that, sir!" Fred warned as he backed away. "She's a fighter, she is. An' wot a temper on 'er! An' she's apt ter cry the 'ouse down!"

Busy with the cord that secured her, his master did not reply. In a few minutes he had her hands loose. Not even thinking of what she did, Penelope made a tight fist and struck him in the face as hard as she could.

Howling, he jumped away, as Fred said, "Tole ye she were a nasty one, guv'ner. Warned ye, I did."

"Oh, go away," the other man said, rubbing his jaw. "I daresay she is only upset at the way she has been treated. Can't blame her."

As the groom hesitated, he waved an impatient hand. "Go on, now! I can handle her myself, and perhaps she might feel more the thing if you were not here to remind her of the unpleasant time she's been having."

As Fred moved to the door, he called after him. "Do not dismiss the carriage. I think I'm going to need it again shortly."

Penelope heard the groom's muttered assent and the door closing behind him, before his master said, "Now, you listen to me, child! I'm quite willing to free you from the rest of your bonds, remove that gag as well, but I must have your promise that you will not scream, or attempt any more violence. Since I'm not in the habit of striking females, you have me at a distinct disadvantage. Just nod, if you agree, and I promise you, you'll soon feel more comfortable."

Still frowning, Penelope breathed deeply through her nose. It did not take her long to realize that she really had no other choice, and, grudgingly, she nodded.

"Good!" he said as he came within range again and pushed a chair behind her. "Here, do sit down and let me untie your feet. And then, of course, remove the gag. I do apologize for my servants. They had no idea they were taking the wrong person, you know. And when all is said and done, you were not harmed, now, were you? In a little while, all this will be over, and you'll not only be returned to your village, but perhaps be able to laugh at your adventure as you enjoy the money I am prepared to give you for your trouble."

All the time he had been speaking, he had been busy with the cord and the gag, and free of that restraint at last, Penelope took a deep, steadying breath. "No, I really do not think my laughing at it at all likely, sir," she said.

Although his face fell, his fair brows rose at her educated accents. "Now we're in the suds!" he muttered, as if to himself. "Gentry, by all that's holy!"

Penelope was rubbing her wrists, trying to restore the circulation to them, and she ignored him, for her mind was working furiously. He had told the groom to keep the carriage ready, so he must mean to return her. But perhaps it would be better if he did not know who she was? Yes, certainly! For that way, her name would not be sullied, and neither would her family's. She vowed she would not tell him anything. Anything at all.

"Should you care for a glass of wine?" her unwitting kidnapper asked, his voice deferential. "No, better not at your age. Some tea or coffee perhaps?"

"Coffee would be very welcome," Penelope told him at her haughtiest, trying to forget how hungry she was. Without a proper dinner the evening before, and no breakfast this morning, she was more than sharp-set.

"Perhaps you would care to retire to freshen up a bit?" he asked next. "There's an anteroom adjoining you could use."

Penelope said nothing, and he colored up a little at her unwavering glare as he said, "I fear you are a bit untidy, miss. Er... your hair ..."

Penelope put her hand to her head and discovered that she had lost the ribbon that secured her curls. They were every whichway, and knowing how frightful she must look, she nodded and rose.

"I do not think it wise to summon a maid for you. The fewer people who see you, the better," he said as he hurried to open another door for her at the back of the room. "I hope you will be able to manage without one."

Penelope refused to answer him as she went by him—with her nose in the air—to shut the door firmly behind her. The small room she was in boasted a close stool, as well as a basin of water and a towel. She washed her face, and when she stared into the mirror above the basin, she almost groaned. How dreadful she looked! she admitted. Her eyes were huge with shock, and her hair a tangle of untidy curls straggling over her shoulders in complete disarray. She had no comb, and where her hair ribbon had gone to, she could not say, but she did the best she could with her fingers. It was not very successful, but at last, accepting that it was the best she could do, she went to rejoin her most unwanted host.

He was alone, although the coffee had been brought in her absence. Penelope was delighted to see a plate of biscuits accompanied it. Her host poured her a cup and handed it to her before he took a seat opposite.

"Now, child, you must tell me your name, and how you came to be wearing that scarlet cloak. I cannot imagine why your mother would dress you in such a thing, unless she has no taste at all."

He saw Penelope was looking perplexed, and he added, "I mean . . . er . . . scarlet cannot be said to be at all flattering to your . . . er . . . your hair."

"Horrid orange hair," Penelope remembered he had called it, and she stiffened.

He waited, but when she said nothing, he went on, "Come now. You must tell me where you live— who you are! Otherwise, all I can do is return you to that little village where my grooms found you. And somehow I do not think you live there, do you? Were you merely traveling through? And how came you to have that cloak? It does not even fit you properly, so therefore I must surmise it is not yours after all. Did you steal it?"

"Of course I didn't!" Penelope exclaimed, setting her cup down with a snap. "I merely . . ."

Her lips closed tightly again; she settled back in her chair and folded her arms over her stomach, as if daring him to try and make her say another word.

He sighed and ran a hand through his elegant hair. Penelope noticed he was beginning to look harassed, and she was glad.

They both heard the sound of a carriage as it approached the front of the house, and he got up quickly to hurry to the window. As he held the drapery slightly aside, she heard him groan.

"Damnation! Why does Laurence have to come here now, of all times?" he asked no one in particular. "He must not see you!"

He turned to stare wildly about the room, but there was no hiding place there. "Quickly!" he hissed, coming to take her hand and pull her to her feet. "Get into the anteroom, and whatever you do, don't make a sound! If Laurence discovers you, all will be lost!"

Penelope dug in her heels, trying to resist his efforts to pull her to the door. She could hear voices in the hall now, and she had the happy thought that this new man—whom her kidnapper seemed so apprehensive of—might be just the person to help her. It did not appear the blond one was going to do anything to the point, at all quickly.

"Stop fighting me, and do as you're told!" he said, as if she were no more than two and ten. "As soon as I get rid of him, we'll see about—"

The hall door opened then, and a smooth, cool baritone could be heard saying, "No need to announce me, Banks. M'cousin and I have never stood on ceremony, especially in the country."

Penelope was startled to find herself being thrust down to the floor behind a small sofa.

"Stay there and be quiet!" the blond man ordered in a harsh whisper.

"Why, Laurence! What on earth are you doing here?" he added aloud in a very different tone of voice as he moved away. "I—I had no idea you were even in the neighborhood."

To Penelope, he sounded most uncomfortable, his words contrived, and she was not surprised to hear the newcomer say in some amusement, "Why, can it be there is some reason you don't wish me here, Alastair? But how can that be, dear fellow? If I remember correctly, when we parted in London a few weeks ago, we did so in perfect harmony.

"What have you been up to now? You might just as well confess. I'll have it out of you, y'know. I always do."

"I haven't the foggiest idea what you're talking

23

about," the man named Alastair protested. "But do sit down and let me pour you some wine."

"I think I'd rather have some of that coffee you've been enjoying."

There was a pause, and she heard this Alastair's indrawn breath quite clearly. "Oh, no! Don't sit there, Laurence! It's much too near the fire, and you'll be scorched. Come, sit over here."

"But I prefer this chair," came the steady reply. "Why, how very singular!"

Intrigued, Penelope moved slightly, so she could peek around the edge of the sofa. She saw a tall, well-built man with dark hair staring down at the carpet before him. He was sitting in the chair she had recently vacated.

"Opening a parcel, cuz?" he inquired idly as he drew the cord that had bound her through his big hands. "And here, if I'm not mistaken, is a handkerchief. How came it to get so twisted and damp? And can this be . . . ? Why, yes! A lady's satin hair ribbon!"

Penelope held her breath, waiting for his cousin to explain, but he said nothing.

As the stranger rose and sauntered closer, she shrank back out of sight.

"Come now! Confession is good for the soul, you know! You've been up to no good, now have you? I suspected something was amiss when you left town so hurriedly, and I know that look of yours. You might just as well sport a sign proclaiming your guilt."

"I don't know how you can say so, or make such a to-do about such a little thing!" Alastair blustered. "The housemaid has not been in this morning to clean the room. She must have dropped the ribbon yesterday, and the handkerchief as well. Very sad way she's in, poor girl. Her young man . . . er . . . the Fultons' underbutler, has started to walk out with another maid. That would explain the damp handkerchief. Been crying over him, I imagine."

"She must have wept an ocean of tears . . . for it still to be damp twenty-four hours later," his guest said dryly. "But I congratulate you on your inventiveness. How will you explain the cord, I wonder?"

There was a short silence, and then his host began to bluster again. "I've no idea where that came from! A man can't explain everything, you know!"

"Or even, I fear, *anything*," his cousin retorted. "But I believe you were going to order coffee?"

Penelope peeked out again as Alastair went to the bellpull. When she dared to look at the stranger, she held her breath. He was staring at his cousin's back with a dark look on his face, and for some reason, she was frightened. He looked so hard, almost cruel.

When Alastair returned from giving the butler orders, Penelope saw the nervous way he darted a glance at the sofa she was hiding behind, as if to make sure she was still safely hidden away. When he saw her peeking around the end of it, he glared at her, then coughed as he took his former seat.

"Are you quite sure *you* were not the one who has been dallying with the housemaid? Then thought better of it and gave the girl her congé?" his cousin inquired. "I only mention it as a possibility, you know . . . because of that large bruise you sport. A fresh one, too, I see," he added as he raised his quizzing glass in inspection.

Alastair's hand flew to his cheek. "Oh, that," he said, trying for an airy tone as he crossed one well-breeched knee over the other and leaned back at his ease. "Walked into a door this morning. Deep in thought, y'know. Didn't notice where I was going."

"I had hoped Gentleman Jackson had cured you

of that bad habit you have of leading with your chin, but let it go," his cousin murmured.

After that, until the coffee had been served and the butler bowed himself away, he spoke only of inconsequential things: some current gossip, the clement weather, reports of family and friends. But when the door closed behind the butler at last, he dropped his casual air and said quite sharply. "It won't do, Alastair. It won't do at all! But before we go any further, perhaps the young lady hiding behind the sofa might be persuaded to come out? It cannot be very comfortable for her, crouched there on the floor."

For several moments, there was a deathly silence in the library. Penelope waited, thinking this Alastair might say something, but when he did not, she scrambled to her feet to face both gentlemen.

"Good heavens!" she heard the newcomer exclaim as he took in the startling sight of tumbled red curls topping a scarlet cloak, huge dark blue eyes set wide in a pale face, even the little freckles on the bridge of Penelope's nose.

"It's not at all what you think, Laurence," her host began hastily. "Silly sort of mix-up, is all—and one you don't want to get involved in, I assure you! The young lady is here by mistake . . ."

"I'm sure that is so. She's not at all to your taste," his cousin remarked as he rose and bowed. "Won't you join us, Miss . . . er . . . ?"

"She wouldn't tell me her name!" Alastair muttered. "Doubt if she'll tell you, either. Stubborn piece! Can't get a civil word from her . . . 'pon my soul, you can't!"

Penelope stood very still while the strange gentleman regarded her with a quizzical look. Angry at being observed so intently, she put up her chin and moved forward. His smile as she did so took her by surprise, for it quite transformed his forbidding face.

"Please sit down," he invited, setting a chair for her between them. "This is your cup? More coffee?"

Penelope nodded, concentrating on keeping her hands from trembling.

"Cream? Sugar? No?" he continued before he handed it to her.

"Now, Alastair, I'll have the whole story," he said as he took his seat again and stirred his own coffee. "As the head of the family, I do have the right to insist on it."

"Oh, very well," his cousin muttered. "I can see I'll get no peace until I tell you!

"I've been looking for someone—no, you don't know her!—and my grooms brought this girl here in error. That cloak she wears was familiar to them, and they thought her the woman I seek. But it was all just a dreadful mistake."

"I hardly think kidnapping can be considered only a 'dreadful mistake,' sir—and I am sure any justice would agree with me," Penelope dared to say.

"Justice?" Alastair said, his voice horrified. "No, no! There is no need for the law!"

"I hope I can persuade your young lady to that view," his cousin said before he sipped his coffee.

"She's *not* my young lady!"

"And wouldn't be for all the wealth of the Indies!"

"Children, children! Cry peace!" the older gentleman murmured, amused. "We shall never get to the bottom of this if you continue to brangle!

"Since neither of you appears to be at all forthcoming, I shall have to reconstruct this morning's events by myself," he added. "But first, might I suggest you remove that cloak, ma'am? You must

27

be very warm wearing it indoors, and besides, it really does not flatter you."

His words were accompanied by that wonderful smile, and when he stood up and came over to her, holding out his hands to receive the garment, Penelope found herself taking it off and handing it to him, meek as any lamb.

The gentleman cast a quick, knowing eye over her slight figure in a kerseymere gown. The gown was hardly in the first stare of fashion, but neither was it one a servant might wear. He laid the cloak over a chair and took his seat again.

"Now," he said, "one must surmise that your grooms used force, cuz, and tied the young lady up and gagged her. Bad form, that. Very bad form."

"They had no choice! Brown tells me she fought hard, and she was trying to scream for help."

"Most understandable, don't you think? She must have been frightened out of her wits."

He turned to Penelope then, and said, "My congratulations, ma'am. I know few females who would not have gone off into a deep swoon—after having hysterics, of course. You have quite extraordinary courage."

Penelope had meant to remain haughty and aloof, but when she saw the twinkle in his eyes, she was forced to smile a little in return.

"Where did your grooms find her?" he asked his cousin next.

"Some little village less than a day's journey from London," Alastair admitted.

His cousin turned back to Penelope. "Can you at least tell me what time of the morning you were abducted, ma'am?"

Penelope considered for a moment, but since she did not think the information would harm her, she said gruffly, "Shortly after six, sir."

"You were up and about early!"

"I only wanted to take a walk before . . ."

Both gentlemen waited, but she folded her lips in a tight line and said no more.

"I see," the elder mused, caressing his chin. "It is now eleven. She has been here how long, Alastair?"

His cousin looked at the Cartel clock on the mantel; his fair brows rose. "Why, less than an hour! Strange, that! It seems much longer."

"For her, too, I'm sure," the older gentleman remarked, his voice carefully expressionless. "So, this village is about a four-hour drive from here? Well, I do not see any problem then. We have simply to order your carriage, and escort Miss . . . er . . . the young lady back to where she was first apprehended. I cannot tell you how relieved I am!"

"Why?" Alastair asked, looking confused.

"Because if it had been impossible for us to return her until tomorrow, or even after dark today, she would be ruined. And in that case, I am sure her parents or her guardians, as the case may be, could very well insist you marry her."

Three

"WE MUST LEAVE at once!" two horrified voices cried in unison. The dark-haired gentleman laughed in genuine amusement. "No, no. There is no need for such haste. It will not be dark for hours yet. And if, as I suspect, the young lady did not have a chance to breakfast this morning, she must be hungry.

"Cuz, why don't you request an early repast? Perhaps served in here? We can be on our way later."

"I shall do so right away," Alastair exclaimed, hurrying to the door. "And I'll order the carriage brought round in half an hour."

"Better make that an hour. I've told you there is plenty of time, and you would not be so discourteous as to rush your ... er ... your guest through her meal, now would you?"

It was perhaps fortunate that Alastair had already left the room—and so did not have to answer that remark.

Alone with the other gentleman, Penelope began to feel uneasy. Her heart was beating rapidly again, and her breathing was erratic. To her relief, the man only gave her an absentminded little smile before he wandered over to a window to stare out at the grounds.

Penelope did not know whether to feel relieved or annoyed. She had thought he would try to question her further, and although she had no intention of telling him, or his odious cousin, a single thing, somehow she could not like being ignored.

When Alastair returned, he found the two preserving an unbroken silence. "See, I told you she wouldn't tell you anything," he remarked to his cousin.

"So you did. But I have not been asking her anything. I never waste time engaging in futile endeavors. All is in train?"

"Banks will bring the luncheon himself. I wish it were possible to avoid having him see her, but . . ."

"Nothing could be simpler. She can retreat to the antechamber while all is being made ready, and certainly we can serve ourselves for once, don't you think?

"Perhaps you had better retire there now, ma'am? This is your hair ribbon I found? Good! I shall lend you my comb, since I see you do not have your reticule with you."

Penelope rose and curtsied a little. "Thank you," she said in real gratitude.

It took her quite a while to tame her unruly locks, and she did not hurry the task. She told herself she had no desire to spend a minute more than she had to with either gentleman.

But even though she was so hungry her stomach hurt, she still wished they could have left immediately. Not because if she failed to reach her aunt's protection by sundown she might be forced to marry this person. She would never do that, never! Better social ruin! But because every minute she was gone was painful for her sister, and, of course, for her aunt Eliza. And she had been missing for hours now! What must they be thinking? Doing? Had they set the law to find her? she wondered, hoping they had not. The fewer people to know of this debacle, the better. And if they had taken no action, she might still escape from the coil she found herself in, with no damage done. Except to Phillipa's nerves, that is, she reminded herself grimly. Poor Phil!

At last she heard the butler enter the library and begin setting the table there, and only a little while later, a knock on the anteroom door told her she might come out now.

She found both gentlemen waiting courteously by a table that had been set in the bow window. The blond one gave her only a cursory glance, but as she held out the other's comb to him, he smiled at her, as if in approval. Penelope was annoyed to find herself blushing.

As he helped her to her chair, that man said, "But how could I have been so remiss? Allow me to introduce myself and my cousin, ma'am."

"Don't see that," Alastair muttered as he spread his napkin in his lap. "She won't say who *she* is. Why should we?"

"Because not to do so would be boorish, and neither of us is a boor. But perhaps I should speak only for myself?"

His cousin flushed a little. Penelope saw that his bruised jaw was darkening, and she was glad.

"I am Laurence Russell, Marquess of Thornbury, and this is my cousin, Mr. Alastair Pettibone, ma'am. Do allow me to help you to some chicken."

Confused, Penelope nodded. A marquess? Good heavens! She congratulated herself on keeping her own counsel, even as she wondered if he knew her uncle William.

"Do pass our Miss X the salad, Alastair," the marquess suggested.

Penelope thought his suggestions were more like orders, but she was so hungry she could only approve. The chicken in a wine-mushroom sauce was delicious, as was the delicate poached salmon, and the rolls had obviously been baked only hours before. For a while she ate steadily, her eyes on her plate, and conversation languished. But at last, replete, she put down her fork and sighed.

She saw her reluctant host looking rather astonished at the amount she had tucked away, but she had no intention of blushing for it. After all, she told herself, her hunger was all his fault!

When the carriage drove up to the front of the house, Mr. Pettibone rose hastily, although the marquess lingered over his wine.

"Surely we should be on our way now, Laurence," his cousin said impatiently.

The marquess shrugged. "Very well. You'll be in a positive fret otherwise."

He went to fetch Penelope's cloak from where he had laid it earlier. She saw him grimace as he came toward her, and when she rose she was trembling again. She could not know that he was comparing the scarlet of the cloak to the rich abundance of curls clustered on her head. The sunlight streaming in through the window behind her, turned them to flame. The cloak looked very tawdry in comparison.

"I am so sorry you must don this most inappropriate garment again, ma'am, but I think it best. And if you pull the hood well forward, it will hide your face and hair."

"Thank you," Penelope whispered as he put it over her shoulders. "It is considerate of you to have such a care for my reputation, m'lord."

"Let me escort you to the carriage, now. We will join you there shortly," he said, holding out his arm after she had adjusted the large hood.

As they left the library and walked through the hall, Penelope kept her eyes on the floor. She sensed there were others there. The butler? A footman, perhaps? but she did not look up until she

33

reached the carriage. The marquess helped her to a seat and shut the door behind her before he disappeared into the house again.

"Hurry, hurry!" Penelope whispered, thinking of her sister's distress. "Let us be gone!"

As she waited, drumming her fingers on the seat, she saw two horsemen cantering up the drive; she shrank back in a desperate attempt to escape notice.

One of the men peered in at her as he halted his horse near the steps, but Penelope did not see, for she was staring down into her lap, praying the hood concealed her features.

"I say, Alastair. Going someplace?" she heard a strange, deep voice ask.

"As you see, Bart," he said, sounding harassed. "Sorry to dash off like this when you have just arrived, but the matter is urgent. Most urgent! Oh, and my apologies to you as well, Feathers."

"And here is your cousin. Well met, Thornbury. Haven't seen you this age. Never tell me you're off, too," the stranger said.

" 'Fraid I am. I must bear my cousin company," the marquess replied in his easy voice.

"I told you we should have sent word of our coming, Bart—but if you remember, you said there was no need," a light tenor voice complained.

"No matter. We have had a pleasant ride, in any event. I'll look for you another day, Alastair."

There was silence for a moment, until Mr. Pettibone said nervously, "Please, do not let us keep you. Give you good day."

"Oh, no, of course not," his visitor replied. "Safe journey to you."

Penelope heard them turn their horses and trot off, and only then did she dare look up. Moments later, the marquess and his cousin joined her inside, the hated grooms who had abducted her jumped to their perch at the rear, and the coach bowled away down the drive.

"Do you think Bart noticed her?" Mr. Pettibone asked abruptly.

"I imagine he did. Bartholomew Whitaker's a downy one. He always has been. And of course there was your own manner, so nervous and abrupt. Bound to wonder about that. What a pity it is you are not a better actor, cuz!"

Turning to Penelope, seated beside him, he said, "How wise of you to keep your face hidden, ma'am. All may still be well."

Penelope nodded, her brow wrinkled in thought. She did not like to confess that for one frightening moment, she had peeked out the window of the coach and caught a tall, loose-limbed gentleman's eye. She remembered how he had stared at her in some astonishment, but she did not mention that. No, for it was almost over. In a few hours she would be reunited with her aunt and her sister, and, hopefully, she would never have to see any of these gentlemen again. Ever.

Much later, as they neared the end of their journey, Penelope began to worry about how she was to discourage her fellow travelers from insisting on meeting her family. She did not want Aunt Eliza to catch a single glimpse of them. How she was to explain her lengthy absence without them, she did not know, but she told herself she would worry about that later.

Perhaps she could suggest they put her down on the outskirts of the village? Somehow she was sure Mr. Pettibone would be only too happy to comply with such a request, but she rather doubted his cousin the marquess would agree.

She had read his character correctly. As the

coach neared the village and she ventured to suggest her plan, he looked severe.

"Of course we will do no such thing as set you down in the road, ma'am," he said, sounding as if she had insulted his standing as a gentleman. "What a pair of loose screws you must think us!"

"But—but it will be so difficult to explain! And if you are not in sight, my . . . er . . . my . . ."

Mr. Pettibone looked frightened. "Here, I say!" he exclaimed. "You don't have a hot-to-hand brother waiting for you, do you? Or perhaps a crusty old father very high in the instep?

"I say, Laurence. Perhaps we had better do as she says . . ."

"Henhearted, Alastair?" the marquess drawled. "We shall do no such thing. And if we do run into any angry male relatives of our Miss X's, let that be a lesson to you.

"Ah, I perceive we have reached the village proper. You must direct us, ma'am."

Penelope unclasped the hands she had been clenching in her lap and turned them upward in defeat. "Go to the inn, m'lord," she said gruffly.

The marquess tapped on the roof, and when the coachman opened the trap, gave him their destination. Penelope saw m'lord did not look as if he approved of the inn when they drove into its muddy yard moments later. She could hardly wonder at it. Even in the pleasant late afternoon sunlight, it still looked mean.

"You have been staying *here*?" Alastair Pettibone asked in astonishment.

As Mr. Pettibone dawdled after them, the marquess led her to the door of the inn, calling for the landlord as they stepped into the grimy hall.

The same beetle-browed, gray-haired man that Penelope remembered hurried from the taproom. When he saw Penelope, he grimaced.

"Ah, no," he said firmly. "Not again! I won't 'ave ye in the 'ouse, miss, and that's final!"

"Whatever do you mean?" the marquess demanded. He sounded so harsh that Penelope did not wonder that the landlord cringed a little.

"I means this one's nothin' but trouble, thass what I mean," he managed to say, screwing up his courage. "No end o' branglin' an' wranglin' there was this mornin', all 'cause she disappeared. An' what with the mean old bit demandin' the law, an' the young one screamin' and cryin' an' fallin' into one swoon after 'tother, me poor rib was run off her feet tryin' ter calm 'em. As fer that other female— well! I never thought no gentry mort would even know the words she used, an' at the top o' 'er voice, too, I might add. Half the village could 'ear 'er. It were a disgrace!"

The marquess ignored Penelope's soft moan. "It seems peaceful enough now," he observed.

Indeed, an almost funereal hush hung over the poor establishment, and Penelope's eyes widened. "But where are they?" she whispered.

"Gone," the landlord said in a satisfied voice. "Loped off, the lot o' them, several hours ago—an' good riddance is what I say."

"Oh, no," Penelope groaned, one hand to her cheek.

The marquess looked down at her and whispered, "Courage!" Aloud he said, "And where exactly did they . . . er . . . lope off to?"

The landlord shrugged. "Don't know an' don't care. But I 'spect they went ter Lunnon. Took the road south, anyways. An' that there fancy gentry mort was 'ot in pursuit the last I seed. Tole 'em they'd not think they could get away, for she meant to 'ave 'er cloak back if she 'ad ter go ter the law. 'Ad ter wear missy's gray one, she did, an' that furious she was!"

"Louisa!" Mr. Pettibone breathed. "It *was* her! She *was* here!"

"I rather think I shall be forced to bespeak a private parlor, and some wine," the marquess said in a voice that brooked no argument. "This must all be thought upon. But no, no wine," he added, looking around the dingy hall and grimacing. "Some of your home brew, and a glass of lemonade for the lady."

"Ain't got no lemonade," the landlord told them, sounding pleased.

"Never mind. I—I don't care for anything," Penelope said in a little voice. Gone! her mind kept repeating. They were gone, and without her, too. For a moment, she was so angry at being abandoned in such a cavalier fashion that she wanted to throw something. Aunt Eliza knew she didn't have a penny with her. How could she *do* such a thing?

Suddenly she thought of something, and she said, "Did my—Er . . . did one of them leave something for me? A package or a letter?"

The landlord stared at her for a moment before he nodded. "Aye, that old mean 'un did. I'll fetch it fer ye."

"The parlor first," the marquess said firmly as he took Penelope's arm. "I've no intention of standing about in this hall a moment longer than need be."

Grudgingly the man showed them to a small room down the hall. It was badly furnished, but at least it was private. Penelope would have paced up and down, waiting for the letter, if the marquess had not insisted she take a seat.

"He'll return presently, ma'am," he said as he held out a chair for her. "There is no need to upset yourself."

"What I don't understand, and never will, is why your family just decamped," Mr. Pettibone complained. "Seems a dashed odd thing to do. For all they knew you might have been in dire trouble."

"I was," Penelope reminded him, her eyes full of dislike.

"Yes, but—"

"Ah, here is our home brew, and your parcel, ma'am," the marquess interrupted as the landlord came in with a tray. He set a pitcher of ale and two glasses on the table, and handed Penelope a small package wrapped in brown paper and tied with string.

" 'Ere, ye wasn't plannin' on stayin', was ye?" he asked the marquess. " 'Cos I meant what I said, ye know. I'd as lief not 'ave this 'oly terror in me 'ouse."

The marquess raised both his quizzing glass and one dark brow, and the landlord retreated to the door.

"I do assure you we do not stay a moment longer than is absolutely necessary," Thornbury said in an icy voice.

Bowing and pulling his forelock in relief, the landlord backed out and shut the door behind him.

Penelope stared down at the package before her, almost as if she were afraid to open it. Alastair Pettibone stared at her in return.

"Well?" he said. "Aren't you going to see what's in it?"

"Oh. Oh, yes, of course," Penelope said as she struggled with the string. When she had the package open they all saw that it contained a purse and a letter. She peeked into the purse and was relieved to find a small cache of shillings. For a moment, she hesitated, then she took a deep breath and opened the letter. It was not very long. Written by her aunt Eliza, it merely said that since she didn't have the faintest idea where Penelope had gotten herself to—although she was sure she would be all right, for after all, she was a competent girl—she herself was taking poor Phillipa to London and the safety of her uncle's house. Poor Phillipa's nerves were quite devastated, and it was all her heedless sister's fault. She would, she wrote in the manner of one congratulating herself on her forbearance, say nothing of the state of her *own* nerves. She also wrote she did not think she could ever find it in her heart to forgive her niece for the trouble she had brought upon them, nor for the number of shillings that should never have had to be squandered in this fashion. Penelope was bidden to be as frugal with the money as possible, for her aunt expected a strict account of them. She was told to remain at the inn. No doubt her uncle would send a carriage for her. And if she had come to woe, it served her right, so difficult and rebellious as she had always been! The letter was not signed.

Ignoring her aunt's cold petulance, Penelope sat very still, considering what she should do. At least she had some money now, and that was something! But she could not stay here and wait for Uncle William's carriage, even if she had wanted to. Perhaps she could travel by stage?

Except, she realized from the long shadows creeping across the floor, it was very late in the day to be doing that.

"I trust your letter contained good news, ma'am?" the marquess asked, breaking into her tumbling thoughts.

Penelope studied hm. She still had no intention of revealing her identity, but she wondered what she was to do now.

"Yes," she made herself say. "I am to journey on by stage tomorrow to join them."

"The stage does not come through this village," the marquess told her in a bored voice.

"What's to be done with her, then?" Mr. Pettibone asked.

"We'll have to take her wherever she intends to go ourselves," the marquess told him, sounding surprised that he hadn't thought of that obvious solution himself.

"But we can't just go haring off to heaven knows where! I've only a small portmanteau with me," his cousin protested. "Besides, it will be dark soon!"

"Very true," the marquess said as he put down his empty glass and rose to look out the window. "I fear we must put up somewhere overnight."

"If you please, sir, and forgive me for saying so, I wish you would just go away," Penelope said firmly. "There can be no impropriety if you are not with me, either you or your cousin. But perhaps you could drive me to another inn? One where the stage does stop? Then I shall do very well."

"My dear good girl, there is not the least chance of my doing any such thing," the marquess said firmly. "My cousin got you into this fix, and it is now my responsibility, as well as his, to get you out of it. I shall not abandon you, but see you safely home. Wherever home may be."

Not waiting for her to comment, he said, "Was the landlord correct, ma'am? This older woman and the young girl in hysterics—they were going to London?"

When she hesitated, he waved an impatient hand. "Oh, come now! Surely there is no harm in telling me that! London is a very large metropolis."

"Yes, they were going to London," Penelope admitted, stung by his scornful glare.

"I still think it was reprehensible of them to go off and leave a grubby schoolgirl to fend for herself," Alastair Pettibone complained. "She doesn't even have a maid!"

"I am not a schoolgirl, nor am I the slightest bit

grubby!" Penelope protested, flashing him another look of dislike.

"No, you're up to every rig and row in town, I suppose!" Pettibone sneered.

"Finish your ale, cuz. To my great surprise it is not at all despicable," the marquess interrupted. "We must be on our way. Should you care to retire first, ma'am?"

Penelope nodded, and, clutching her precious purse and letter, she left the room.

The marquess waited until the door had closed behind her before he said, "Now let us consider, Alastair. Who do we know in this part of the country?"

His cousin frowned. "Can't say *I* know anybody. But why is that important?"

"Because, dear boy, we must find a safe haven for tonight. As you so rightly pointed out, Miss X has no maid, certainly no chaperon, and neither of us would fill either role. We need to sleep in a respectable house, with a married couple in residence. Think now! There must be someone! We're not that far from St. Albans or Hatfield."

He paused suddenly, caressing his chin in that familiar gesture. "Hmmm," he said. "Hatfield ... Hatfield. Aha! I have it!"

"Have what? Don't know a soul in Hatfield, I assure you."

"Not there! Little Berkhampstead!"

His cousin stared at him perplexed for a moment, and then a horrified look came over his face. "Oh, no you don't, Laurence! I absolutely refuse to go to my great-aunt and -uncle Pettibone's! You know I've been avoiding them for years!"

"It can't be helped. They're the closest, and no one could say they're not the height of respectability, even if they are a trifle ... er ... eccentric."

"A trifle? A trifle?" his cousin demanded, his voice rising. "They're both of them mad as hatters!"

He continued to argue hotly against the scheme, but when Penelope came back into the room, after a futile whispered conversation with the landlord in which she had tried to hire his gig to take her to the nearest market town—and had been most firmly refused—the marquess told her they were taking her to an estate near Little Berkhampstead, where she would be quite safe and more than adequately chaperoned. Tomorrow, they would travel on to London.

He seemed to consider the matter settled, but then, he did not know Miss Penelope Shaw.

Four

LADY ELIZA AND Miss Shaw had arrived in London
several hours earlier that day, the older lady in a
state of deep resentment and chagrin, and the younger, a bundle of quivering, ragged nerves. Lady
Eliza's vinaigrette had come into play more than once
on the journey, and she herself had had occasion to
resort to the emergency bottle of brandy as well. By
the time they reached their relative's home, Phillipa
had cried herself out, although she still had to be
supported into the house by the groom.

William Shaw's able butler took in the situation
at a glance, and after sending one of the footmen
for the housekeeper, suggested Lady Eliza and her
niece retire to a nearby salon to compose themselves while they waited for their rooms to be prepared. Perhaps they would care for tea?

"Tea? Certainly not! I'll have a glass of sherry,
Tuttle!" the older lady said firmly. "Better bring one
for Miss Phillipa as well. The things we have been
forced to endure! It does not bear thinking about!

"Where is my brother?" she added, as Phillipa
moaned and trembled anew.

"I regret to say His Grace is from home, ma'am,"
the butler said as he led the way to the salon. "I
shall, of course, apprise him of your arrival as soon
as he comes in."

"He must be sent for immediately, wherever he is!
We cannot wait," the older lady said as she tottered

into the room and collapsed on a sofa. "Send the footmen running to find him. This is an emergency!"

Wisely, Mr. Tuttle did not argue the point. He had had many dealings over the years with the duke's younger sister, but he had never seen her in such a state as this. He opened his mouth to inquire where Miss Penelope was—and just as quickly closed it. It had been his understanding that the younger Miss Shaw was to have accompanied her aunt and sister to London for the Season. That she had not done so, gave him all kinds of possibilities to consider. Perhaps it was Miss Penelope who was the "emergency"? he wondered as he bowed himself away to fetch the sherry and send the footmen scurrying to the duke's clubs. He had heard of some of her exploits in the past, and he would not be a bit surprised if it were to be so.

Since William Shaw had not frequented any of his clubs that day, the footmen returned without news of him, and it was very late in the day before that elderly personage arrived home to dress for dinner.

Informed by his butler that his sister and niece had arrived, and the former had asked to see him the instant he came in, his thin white brows rose.

"Indeed, Tuttle?" he asked. "And where is my sister now?"

"Lying down in a darkened room, Your Grace. It was necessary to fetch the doctor for Miss Phillipa, she was in such a state of nerves. I believe your niece is sleeping now, thanks to the draught the doctor gave her."

"Laudanum, no doubt. Whatever did our female ancestors do without it?" the duke murmured.

"Well, I shall await my sister in the library. Pray send her to me, if she is able to come, that is."

It was only a matter of minutes before Lady Eliza joined him there. Barely giving him time to greet her and beg her to be seated, she began her story. She

45

spoke uninterrupted, for the duke knew her very well—and realized that to ask for some small clarification, would only delay matters endlessly.

"And as for why she went out, or where she was when we were forced to leave that horrid inn, I have no idea!" Lady Eliza finished at last. "I tell you, William, that girl will be the death of me ... indeed she will! My heart has been palpitating so, I fear the worst, although, of course, I have been so taken up with poor dear Phillipa's condition, I've scarce had a chance to think of myself!"

Her brother decided there was nothing to be gained from pointing out how remiss Penelope's guardian had been to go off and leave the girl to fend for herself.

"Where is this inn located?" he asked instead. On learning it was in a small hamlet a few miles south of Stanborough, he nodded. "There is nothing to be done then at this hour. You say you left a note for Penelope? Money? We must pray she gets both— and will have the good sense to stay put until I can reach her tomorrow."

As his sister began to sob in a gusty way, he went and patted her shoulder. "There now, Lizzy, none of that! Behave yourself! It will be all right, you'll see. If you remember, Penny seems to have the ability to get out of most dilemmas almost unscathed, and by herself, too. She is the most redoubtable girl!"

His sister sniffed as she dried her eyes on her damp handkerchief. "You needn't sound so admiring, William! Believe me, you wouldn't be if you had been the one who had had the raising of her after dear Philip and Katherine died in that carriage accident when she was only five. She has taken years from my life with her pranks, her stubbornness, and her complete disregard for genteel manners and accepted custom."

Her brother hid a wintry smile. From her young

tomboy days, distinguished by abrasions, broken arms, and black eyes, Penelope Shaw had graduated, not to the demure girlhood her aunt preached to her, but to a willful independence. He sympathized with her so, he had no intention of forcing her to make her debut this spring. Eventually his youngest niece would settle to a woman's place, but that time was not yet. Idly the duke wondered who the man would be to make her see the error of her ways.

After a dinner he shared only with his sister later, he inquired more closely of the incident.

"You say this other woman, this Mrs. Bellings, accused Penny of stealing her cloak, Lizzy?"

His sister shuddered. "I wish you would not remind me of her! The most common sort, although I'm bound to admit she appeared the lady, so soft and well-spoken as she was at first, saying she considered it only Christian to offer to share her bed with Penelope. But the words she used this morning when she discovered her cloak was missing would put even *you* to the blush! I was never so deceived. But there, if that isn't just like Penelope, rushing in where saints would fear to go!

"At least we managed to evade this Mrs. Bellings's pursuit. Her carriage was held up by a large herd of cows and we never saw it again. Thank heavens! We might have had her with us this very evening, screaming and carrying on."

"Oh, I hardly think that likely, Lizzy," the duke said. "Not in *my* house. She wouldn't dare.

"But why did Penny take her cloak?" he continued, frowning now.

His sister held out her pudgy little hands in confusion. "I've no idea; in fact, it quite puzzles me. Since she obviously was intent on leaving the inn, perhaps she confused it with her own, although I'm bound to say I don't know how she could have done that. Her cloak was a ladylike gray and unremark-

47

able, while according to this Mrs. Bellings, hers was a brilliant scarlet. Scarlet, William! That tells you something about her, does it not?"

"I wonder why Penny left the inn," her brother said, refusing to be drawn into yet another discussion of Mrs. Louisa Bellings's character—or lack of it. "But perhaps she was only going for an early morning walk before taking coach again?

"And that reminds me, Lizzy. My head groom told me—when I spoke to him about having my carriage ready to leave at dawn—that you came up to town in that fusty old coach that belonged to our grandmother. I wish you had not! It is to make you a laughingstock, to say nothing about what it does to my reputation! And you know very well I have instructed you, time out of mind, to purchase a new one."

"It is a perfectly good coach," Lady Eliza argued, her bosom swelling in indignation. "There is no sense spending money just to be fashionable."

"But how about comfortable?" her brother persisted.

He saw Lizzy was getting her mulish look, and he sighed. He had never understood why, of the six of them, Lizzy had turned into such a clutch-fist. She had a generous portion; indeed, she was a wealthy woman, even though she had never married. And she had her nieces' ample allowances as well. He saw to that. But he could never get her to spend a groat more than she had to. Eyeing her old-fashioned, slightly faded gown, he decided he must find someone else to take his nieces shopping for their town finery. If it were left to Lizzy, she would have haunted the poorer stalls dotted about the less fashionable parts of town searching for bargains, and set his maids to sewing, and that would never do. I wonder if Deirdre would help? he

48

mused as his daughter-in-law's merry face came to mind. She's bang up to the mark.

Resolving to ask her as soon as he returned to London with Penelope, he took a courteous leave of his sister, excusing himself from any more of her affronted ramblings on account of his early start on the morrow.

The duke arrived at the little village Lady Eliza had told him about well before noon the following day. As he descended to the muddy yard of The Fox and Grapes on his groom's arm, he looked around in affronted amazement. Of all the unsuitable places, he thought. Lizzy's doing, of course!

The landlord had been looking from a taproom window, and his eyes under their beetle brows widened at the smart black carriage with its gold trim and the crest on the door, its matched team of thoroughbred horses and liveried grooms and coachman. But he would not have had to even see it to recognize at a glance, when the duke finally came inside, that here was an important personage, born to command and of the highest rank. The bow he gave this gentleman was deep and worshipful, and his wife, who had come from the kitchen to see who had arrived, was struck dumb with awe.

"An' wot might I be doin' fer ye, sir?" he asked eagerly, bowing again.

William Shaw raised his handkerchief to his nose. The stench of sour spilled ale, cooking, and smoke was most unpleasant. "I am here to fetch my niece, Miss Penelope Shaw," he said. "I believe she stayed here with her aunt and sister two nights ago . . . and somewhat mysteriously disappeared. I trust she has returned by now?"

The landlord took a small step backward. "But— but she's not 'ere, sir!" he breathed.

The duke bent a stern eye on his cowering figure. "Where is she then?" he asked.

The landlord shrugged. "No idea, an' that's the truth, sir. She did come back, late yestiddy afternoon it were, but almost at once she was off again with them two swells."

" 'Swells'?" the duke echoed, raising his white brows. "I fear you must be more plain."

No sign of the unease he felt showed in either his face or his voice, but then William Shaw had lived some sixty-one years and could be as imperturbable as a clam when he chose.

"Aye, sir. It's as me 'usband says," the innkeeper's wife volunteered, and then, as the duke transferred his gaze to her face, rather wished she hadn't.

"They come together in a coach, they did, and bespoke a private parlor. But they didn't stay," she hurried to add.

One can certainly understand why, the duke thought to himself. Aloud, he said, "Did she receive the money and the letter my sister left for her?"

"Ter be sure," the landlord said, happy to be able to relate some good news. " 'Anded it ter 'er meself, I did! An' then, she come out o' the parlor alone an' tried ter 'ire me gig ter take 'er ter the nearest market town where she could catch the stage. But I wouldn't let 'er 'ave it, no, sirree! That one, beggin' yer pardon, sir, is a 'oly terror! Such trouble as she brought ter the 'ouse. Why—"

The duke waved an impatient hand. "I am aware. But did no one mention their destination? The two gentlemen . . . er . . . swells, perhaps?"

"Mebbe Jeb over'eard somethin', 'Arry," the innkeeper's wife contributed. " 'E's the ostler, sir."

The duke agreed that Jeb should be fetched at once, and until he arrived at a dead run from the stable, an uneasy silence was observed. Jeb appeared so in awe of the duke he could not speak, but at last, after a great deal of prodding, he did manage to stutter that he thought he had heard one of them fine gents mention Little Berkhampstead when he was giving instructions to his coachman. The ostler was duly rewarded with a coin, and he backed away, almost falling off the steps in his hurry to be gone.

The duke was not at all loathe to follow his example, leaving the innkeeper and his wife bowing and curtsying to him as if he were King George himself.

As his carriage left the inn yard, William Shaw permitted himself a ferocious scowl. It was bad enough that Penny had been accompanied by two men, but that she had gone off with them again, instead of staying at the inn as she had been told to do by her aunt, astounded and upset him.

And why had she tried to hire the innkeeper's gig? Were those men holding her against her will? And where had she been all day yesterday? Last night? And where was she now?

When he reached Little Berkhampstead later, the duke set his grooms to questioning anyone they found abroad in the lanes of the village, but to no avail. Not a single soul had seen a red-haired girl dressed in a scarlet cloak.

At last, realizing it was futile to waste any more time, the duke gave the order to return to town. No one had seen Penny, but perhaps the ostler had misunderstood? He had not appeared to have too much intelligence.

But as he traveled back to London, William Shaw wondered what he was to do now. He had the greatest reluctance to bring the Runners into the matter, for such a move would mean it would all get out, and Penny's reputation would be ruined. Finally he decided to wait a day or so, hoping she would turn up, and he prayed silently that he had not been mistaken in the girl. He had always thought her as smart as a whip, and he was sure if anyone could extricate herself from an unpleasant situation, it would be his youngest niece.

It was not until his carriage reached the outskirt villages of London that he considered what Lizzy and Phillipa's reaction would be when he showed up without Penny, and he shuddered.

Had the duke but known it, his niece was even then making her own way to town, perched high on a cart filled with firewood. The cart was driven by a farmer who had his wife seated beside him on the perch. Their two young sons sat behind with Penny, who regaled them with stories, songs, and riddles. It was not a comfortable ride, but she considered herself lucky to have it.

All the way to Little Berkhampstead the previous afternoon, she had been planning an escape. It was not only that she knew she should not remain in the marquess and his cousin's company, it was because she didn't want them to take her to London, find out where her uncle lived, and her name. For if they had that information, a careless word from one of them would mean scandal. And after listening to Alastair Pettibone's inane chatter for several hours, she was sure the story would be all around his clubs in a matter of hours. She did not think Laurence Russell would be so careless; he seemed a sensible man, and a kind one, too. Several times he had inquired as to her comfort, and the conversations he held included her as well as his cousin. Still, even though for some inexplicable reason she felt safe with him, she was desperate to escape. How she was to do that, she had no idea, but with the optimism of youth, she was sure something would occur to her.

When she met Alastair Pettibone's elderly relatives at their estate, called Milfield, she forgot her dilemma, for they were so funny, it was all she could do not to laugh in their faces.

They were both tall and thin to the point of gauntness, and they looked more like twins than husband and wife. But it was not their looks that made Penny want to giggle. No, it was because they were both of them deaf—and they didn't seem to have the least notion of their failing.

On first hearing the marquess's explanation of their uninvited call and their need to remain overnight, an explanation that bore not the slightest resemblance to the truth, Penny noted, Elizabeth Pettibone said, "The poor, dear child!"

"It certainly has been mild this spring, but what has that to say to anything?" her husband demanded. "Not that I couldn't agree with you more."

"Well, if she snores, we'll just have to give her a room some distance from our own," his wife replied.

"Broom? Broom? Surely there is no question of putting the young lady to work!"

"What do you mean, berserk, Winston? You don't even know her! Shame on you!"

"Of course I don't *blame* her! No doubt she cannot help it. And if Laurence and Alastair assure us she is not dangerous, well . . ."

"So we are in agreement, husband? The young lady may stay here as long as she likes?"

"Yes, there are some very pleasant hikes to be had in the surrounding countryside. Do you enjoy walking, child?"

The marquess decided it was time to take a hand when he saw his charge's face getting redder and redder till she looked like she was about to burst. It was not a bit flattering with her hair and that scarlet cloak. Besides, if she broke into uncontrollable laughter, the Pettibones were sure to think her mad—and might well reconsider allowing them to stay. That would never do, for he knew no one else in the neighborhood.

Loudly and slowly, he said, "Thank you both. It is good of you to put us up."

"Kindly do not shout, Laurence!" Mrs. Pettibone scolded, frowning now. "Why, anyone would think we were hard of hearing!"

"Yes, we must hope the clearing weather continues, must we not?" her husband contributed. "But perhaps we should have a maid show the young lady to her room. What did you say her name was, Alastair?"

"She is Miss Smith. Miss Abby Smith," the marquess said firmly. "The cousin of a friend of ours."

Penny wished he had allowed her to choose her own alias. Abby Smith was so plain! Why, she would have called herself Rowena Witherspoon, or Cecily Faringham, or something, she thought as she followed the maid to a large upstairs bedchamber. The maid seemed a bit stunned that miss had no baggage, and Penny was forced to invent a story of portmanteaus going astray due to stupid grooms who had taken her carriage on to London without her.

"But there is no need to repine," she told the maid cheerfully as that woman tended the fire. "I shall be home tomorrow, no harm done. Although I admit it would be nice if I had a change of clothes."

She thought she had carried it all off very well, but she could see the maid still thought it singular. But perhaps it was only that scarlet cloak? Everyone seemed to stare at it so!

At dinner later, she was glad the marquess took charge of most of the conversation, talking to the Pettibones of family news and society. Their misunderstanding him and unrelated replies added piquancy to the meal, although Penny was careful never to have her mouth full when they spoke, lest she choke.

Across from her, Alastair Pettibone brooded into his wineglass, deep in thought, but she was surprised to see Laurence Russell studying her more than once, an arrested expression on his stern face. She wondered why he did so; it made her most uncomfortable.

That evening as they went in to dinner she learned that the elderly Pettibones had some peculiar hobbies. When she questioned the marquess about a statue in the hallway that was draped in a sheet he told her Elizabeth Pettibone had the greatest dislike for the nude figure and had covered everything portraying it when she first arrived here as a bride some fifty years before.

"Be sure to notice the oil painting of one of the earlier Pettibones in the drawing room," he whispered. "The lady portrayed is wearing a very low-cut gown. Mrs. Pettibone has added a lace scarf up to the chin. I believe she also endeavored to drape all the suits of armor in the house, but was finally dissuaded, and that the marriage nearly came to tragedy over the natural state her husband allows his dogs."

Penny grinned. "You mean she wanted him to put *clothes* on them?" she whispered.

Laurence Russell nodded solemnly, but at her hastily stifled laugh, he was forced to grin himself.

During the dessert course, Mrs. Pettibone told Penny of her special interest. She was fascinated by spiders, and had several exotic specimens from all over the world that she kept in a special room. She promised to show them to Miss Smith on the morrow, including her prize, a giant tarantula that she had nicknamed Algernon.

Penny smiled and tried to look intrigued rather than repelled.

Mr. Pettibone's particular study was of rocks, which seemed a lot safer, although Penny learned he also bred bulldogs when he warned her she must not leave her room for any reason after they had all retired for the night.

"Let three of them into the house then, to patrol it," he said, nodding to her. "No need for you to feel the slightest unease here, Miss Smith! My dogs are trained to attack strangers."

"The Pettibones have the greatest fear of housebreakers," the marquess murmured.

"Oh, they'll break bones, all right," his host said, a satisfied grin creasing his lined face. "And draw blood. Splendid animals, my bulls. Splendid!"

Penny hid a shudder. She had intended to slip away very early tomorrow and make her way to the highroad. From there she was sure she could find a ride to the nearest market town—where she could hire a gig or take a stage to town—long before the marquess and his cousin were even awake. But now she might have to contend with guard dogs. It was too bad.

Later, in her room, she questioned the maid who had been assigned to her about the dogs.

The maid rolled her eyes. "Horrid things they are! Ugly as sin! But at least the master keeps 'em in the kennels except at night."

"When do they return there?" Penny asked in what she hoped was a casual tone.

"At dawn," the girl said as she turned down the bed.

"Are there other dogs . . . er . . . loose in the grounds at night?"

"Aye, but the keeper calls them in then, too. You may have noticed the entire estate is fenced. That's for them, so they don't get away. Wish they would, sometimes."

Penny thought the maid looked a little wistful, and she wondered if she had a beau the bulldogs were keeping at bay.

By the time the sky began to lighten the next morning, Penny was dressed and ready. She sat near a window in her room, watching the eastern sky for the first sign of the sun. Earlier, impatient as always, she had opened her door a crack, but the sound of three large bulldogs racing up the stairs, their growls very audible, had quickly changed her mind. At last, when she could see clearly, she opened the door cautiously again. There wasn't a sound in the house, and she breathed a sigh of relief. Quickly she tiptoed down the stairs and let herself out. Barely taking time for a deep breath, she sped down the long drive to the front gates, feeling somehow vulnerable in the small of her back, as if an early rising marquess might be peering from his window even then. And in the scarlet cloak she wore, she knew she would be hard to miss.

The gates were locked tight, and Penny almost stamped her foot in frustration. There was no smoke coming from the gatehouse chimney as yet, not that she could ask for help there, of course! Instead, she walked along the fence. Luck was with her, for only a short distance away, at the end of a narrow path through the woods, there was a small, unlocked gate. Perhaps the servants used it as a short cut to the village? she wondered as she let herself out. Surely the Pettibones knew nothing of it.

She herself had no intention of going anywhere near Little Berkhampstead, for it would be the first place the marquess and his reluctant cousin would seek her. Instead, she turned south, toward London. As she strode along, she noticed it was going to be a fine day, and that was fortunate. Rain would have made the entire journey much more unpleasant. And perhaps she would also have good luck finding a ride with some farmer taking eggs and butter to the nearest town.

The fact that she ended up perched on a pile of

firewood didn't bother her at all. She had come upon the farm a few miles away from Milfield, as the farmer and his family were loading the cart. He was a rawboned, taciturn sort, and his wife a little suspicious of Penny, but her smile for their two little boys, and a hastily made up story of why she had to get to London, disarmed them. And when she insisted on paying her way, they were all smiles.

As if fate was smiling at her at last, the farmer was to deliver his wood to his master's town house in St. James's Square; he said he'd be glad to set her down at her uncle's, since Berkeley Square was so close to his own destination.

The pace they traveled was hardly rapid, and Penny knew she would probably not arrive until well after dark. But, she told herself, that was all to the good, for the fewer people to see her and remark her peculiar method of transportation, the better.

And let her aunt Eliza not catch sight of her! she prayed as the little boys dozed off, braced against her on either side.

For although Miss Penelope Shaw was secretly feeling quite proud of herself for the neat way she had managed to extricate herself from a dangerous situation, she was still conscious of qualms of guilt about the suffering her disappearance must have inflicted on her aunt and her sister.

Five

THAT THEY HAD suffered was evident the moment Penny stepped inside her uncle William's house in Berkeley Square. Tuttle, the butler, who had opened the door to her, so forgot himself as to let his mouth fall open in astonishment, and Phillipa's shriek, from where she stood at the top of the stairs, brought more servants into the front hall. It also brought the duke and Lady Eliza.

That gentleman took one look at his niece's unfortunate garb and scowled. But then he set about emptying the hall and restoring order. Phillipa was told to stop making such a cake of herself, although whether the girl heard his lecture was doubtful, for she was clasping Penny in her arms, babbling her relief and crying gustily. As for Lady Eliza, she had sat down abruptly in a chair against the wall, both hands to her heart.

"So, you've arrived at last, have you?" the duke asked, his voice a little grim. "I did not look for you until tomorrow."

"Yes, indeed, and I shall tell you all about it presently, sir," Penny assured him, patting her sister on the back and looking a little harassed. "There now, Phil. Do stop crying and clutching me so! And why are you crying now, when I am safely returned to you?"

"She seems to do nothing *but* cry," the duke remarked dryly. "Worst watering pot I ever saw, 'pon my honor!

"But come into the library, Penny. Tuttle, some supper for my niece, if you would be so good."

As he herded them all before him into his private room and shut the door firmly in the footmen's avid faces, he added, "No need to blurt everything out in front of the servants. Not that they won't find out. They always do."

"Too true," Lady Eliza said gloomily before she rounded on her younger niece. "Oh, you dreadful girl! *Wherever* have you been? And what have you been doing? I'll have the truth, now!"

Penny had known the truth would not serve here, and part of the way to London, she had been busy concocting a story about her early walk—how she had suddenly had a fainting spell and been taken to a nearby farm to recuperate. It was the shabbiest thing, she knew, but it had been all she had been able to think of. And now, as she told it, she saw that although Phillipa believed every word, being so prone to fainting spells herself, her aunt still looked terribly suspicious.

The duke, who had had the sense not to tell his sister of the two gentlemen who were accompanying Penny, had no comment to make at all to her tale.

"You must have really been ill, although I find that hard to believe. You are, in general, so healthy. And you've never fainted in your life," Lady Eliza said when Penny finished at last. "I understand you did not return to the inn until late afternoon? But surely you could have sent a message to me there."

"By the time I was better, it was too late. I must admit I was upset that you and Phil had gone off without me. I never dreamed you would do that!"

Lady Eliza bristled. "And what else was I to do

60

but hurry to town to lay all in my brother's hands? He is a man; it was up to him to find you! And poor, dear Phillipa! I fear her nerves have suffered a permanent shock. It was really heedless of you, Penelope, to go out and then fall ill like that."

"I—I couldn't help it, and indeed, I am sorry that both of you had to worry," Penny managed to say.

"But why didn't you stay at the inn, as you were told?" her aunt asked, leaning forward suspiciously. "Why did you go out again, and where did you go? I will be told! Where did you spend the night?"

"But I couldn't stay there alone, aunt," Penny said swiftly. "And it was such an awful place, I didn't want to. I went back to the farm, of course. They were so kind to me, and Mrs. . . . er . . . Mrs. Smith, the farmer's wife, took such good care of me, even finding me a ride to London on a cart today."

"On a *farmer's* cart? Oh, Penny!" Phillipa wailed in horror.

"It was really quite a lot of fun," Penny reassured her. "Of course, jolting along sitting on firewood for hours and hours was even worse than our old carriage, but I enjoyed the farmer's little boys, and eating a picnic lunch by the roadside."

Tuttle brought her supper in then, and until he left the room there were no more questions.

"Where are my shillings?" Aunt Eliza demanded as soon as they were private again.

Penny stared at her. "Why, I gave some to Mrs. Smith, and the rest to the farmer. After all, he brought me right to the door, and they shared their food with me."

"You gave away twenty shillings, and only for that? Oh, bad, bad girl!" her fond aunt exclaimed. "I'm sure they would have been happy with only one or two."

"Enough, Lizzy!" the duke ordered, and she fell silent in confusion. It was the first time he had spoken, and there was something in his voice that warned her she would be most unwise to continue to harangue her improvident niece.

"So, you arrived in Mayfair perched on a load of firewood in a farmer's cart, did you?" he asked Penny, his voice deceptively mild.

She nodded, studying his austere face for a clue to his feelings.

"We must hope no one saw you, then," he went on. "Although I do not know how you could escape notice in that dreadful garment."

Penny looked down at the scarlet cloak she had yet to remove. She was quick to do so now.

"I don't think anyone saw me, sir," she told him as she laid it over a nearby chair. "There was no one abroad but a footman some doors away, and two gentlemen deep in conversation across the square. And it is late, and so dark."

The duke nodded, and she settled back to enjoy her repast and inspect her surroundings. She had never been to her uncle's before; their meetings had all been in the country at her family home. How very fine this is, she thought, more than a little awed. The massive furniture polished to a high gleam, the rich brocades and velvets of the uphol-stery and hangings, the walls of books, the beauti-ful gold and silver appointments. Her own home was Spartan and shabby in comparison, due to her aunt's frugality. Then and there, Penny decided she preferred opulence.

She glanced at her sister. Phillipa had not taken her eyes from her face, almost as if she were afraid her sister might disappear again if she did. Penny made a funny face at her, and was relieved to see the ghost of a smile in return. When she looked at her aunt Eliza, she was not surprised to see the lady sporting a disgruntled look, her lips moving as if she were mumbling under her breath about those squandered shillings still.

"May I suggest you get rid of that cloak, my dear?" her uncle said in the silence. "It is so jarring with your coloring; why, it is enough to make one shudder."

Penny looked at it critically. "Yes, it is not very nice, is it? I took it by mistake. It was still dark when I dressed and left Mrs. Bellings's room. But I never intended to be gone long."

"Do not mention that woman to me!" Lady Eliza exclaimed. "I doubt she is a married lady; in fact, I doubt she is a lady at all! If you could have heard the things she said, accused us of, Penelope, you wouldn't believe it. And she dared to threaten us with the law, she was so adamant about having her cloak returned."

"Perhaps I should keep it for her," Penny said, after she had disposed of a mouthful of roast beef. "We might see her here in town."

"I'll not have her in this house!" Lady Eliza declared. "And I've given orders to that effect to Tuttle. She will never gain admittance!"

"As you wish," Penny said, resting her head on the velvet back of her chair. She was suddenly, unaccountably weary. Perhaps it was because her hunger had been assuaged and the fire was so warm that her eyes felt heavy, she thought a little dreamily.

She came alert at once, however, when her uncle asked his sister and Phillipa to leave them.

"I've a deal to discuss with Penny," he said as he rose and went to the door to let them out. "You run along now, both of you. I'm sure Penny will be glad to regale you with more of her adventures tomorrow."

Phillipa, who was more than a little afraid of her stern uncle, was quick to scurry from the room.

Lady Eliza looked as if she might be more difficult to budge, until William Shaw reminded her that Phillipa probably needed her attention.

When they were gone, the door closed firmly behind them, the duke came back and took a seat facing Penny. "And now, my good girl, you will tell me what really happened," he said, fixing her with a keen eye. "All those stories you spouted to your aunt and your sister were no better than a Banbury tale, and we both know it! But I'll have the truth right now if you know what's good for you."

Penny had been sure it would come to this, and after considering it on her way to London, had decided there was no escape. The duke had a right to know what had happened, for if he were not enlightened, he might well suspect she had been ruined indeed.

"I know, but those stories were the best I could think of at the time, dear sir," she told him, with a little grin. The duke did not return it, but Penny was not Phillipa, and she did not quake in her boots. Besides, she was really fond of her uncle.

"Perhaps you had better begin by telling me the identity of the two men who accompanied you back to the inn yesterday afternoon," the duke said. "The innkeeper told me of them."

"Wasn't he *awful*?" Penny demanded. "He said he'd not have me in his house. Why, he even called me a holy terror!"

"I quite agree with him on that point. You are one. But those men, Penny?"

His niece's grin faded. "One of them was an Alastair Pettibone. The other was his cousin, Laurence Russell, Marquess of Thornbury."

The duke's expression did not change, and Penny did not see the glint of recognition in his eyes.

"And how came you to be in their care?" he asked.

"It was the strangest thing! Mr. Pettibone had had his grooms out searching the countryside for Mrs. Bellings," Penny told him. "I don't have the vaguest idea why, of course. And when I went for my early walk, those grooms spotted her scarlet cloak. Thinking I was the woman their master sought, they kidnapped me and brought me to his estate."

"Somehow I am sure you did not go willingly," the duke remarked.

"I did not, sir! I fought them as hard as I could, tried to scream, too. But they just tied me up and gagged me."

"And did any of this Mr. Pettibone's servants see you clear when you arrived there? His butler? The maids, for example?"

"No. No one saw me. The groom hoisted me over his shoulder like a sack of meal, and my hood slipped forward over my face. Not even the butler saw me. And tonight, I kept the hood pulled forward as well, as soon as we neared your home."

"Let us be thankful for small blessings," her uncle murmured. Rousing himself a little, he went on, "How came the marquess to be there? Was he also looking for this Mrs. Bellings?"

"No, I don't think he knew anything of her. He arrived to visit while Mr. Pettibone was trying to decide what to do with me. You see, his estate is a four-hour drive from the village where I was taken.

"Of course, when the marquess spotted me hiding behind a sofa, he . . ."

At her uncle's questioning glance, she explained, "Mr. Pettibone pushed me down behind it when his cousin came in."

"This Mr. Pettibone seems a forceful young man, abducting women, pushing them to the floor," the duke remarked grimly.

"Not so very, sir. I managed to plant him a facer when he first untied me. Bruised him good, too!"

"Penny, Penny. Where do you hear such language? It is not at all the thing! No, no. Don't bother to explain. Some stable boy, no doubt. But be warned, all such expressions must be expunged from your vocabulary now you are in town."

Penny agreed meekly enough.

He had many more questions, which she answered freely. During their conversation, he poured them both a glass of wine. Penny sipped hers gingerly. The duke seemed to have forgotten she was only seventeen.

By the time she reached the elderly and eccentric Pettibones and their estate near Little Berkhampstead, William Shaw was having trouble controlling a broad smile.

"I wonder why they have never come my way?" he said in a choked voice when Penny finished describing her hosts. "I should like to meet them; by Jove I would!

"And so you crept away from the house early this morning, did you? But why, girl? It appears the marquess behaved just as he ought, and I am sure he would have brought you to town in perfect comfort."

"That was his intention, but my way was better," Penny said. "You see, I never told them my name, nor where you live. I thought that would protect us all from any gossip. That Alastair Pettibone is so corkbrained, he might well have let something slip, and then the cat would be among the pigeons! Er . . . I mean, I do not think he is a sensible person, dear sir, and I wanted to avoid any trouble."

She yawned broadly then, and the duke rose and pulled her to her feet to hug her briefly. "You had better go off to bed before you fall asleep right in front of me," he said sternly. "We'll talk of all this again tomorrow, and decide what, if anything, needs must be done about it. It does appear, however, that you managed very well, Penny. I was sure you would."

As Penny smiled and curtsied, he considered Alastair Pettibone and his cousin, the Marquess of Thornbury. He knew the family; indeed, he had been friends with the last marquess. Remembering the earlier Laurence Russell, he was glad he had been so sensible—had bred a son much like himself. He must be sure to thank the young man personally for his care of his niece.

That selfsame marquess had spent a frustrating day. On discovering Penny had disappeared, he had had to waste quite a lot of time reassuring the elderly Pettibones as to her character. Still, nothing would do but for both of them to conduct a search of the house to discover which family heirloom or priceless piece of plate she had managed to escape with, for they were sure she must be a thief. Mrs. Pettibone, especially, could not be calmed until she had made sure her precious tarantula was still in his container, and Mr. Pettibone had to personally inspect his rock collection.

To Alastair Pettibone's relief, his cousin did not seem intent on searching for the girl when they finally made their escape in the early afternoon. He had fully expected Laurence to make inquires in Little Berkhampstead, and mentioned this as they went out to the carriage.

"Don't be a fool," came the terse reply. "She won't be there. No, she's on her way to London by now, by hook or by crook. I pray she comes to no harm, for she's as green as grass."

"Then we travel home?" Alastair asked hopefully.

"No, of course we don't! We must go to London as well and make sure she arrived there safely."

"Don't see that," Alastair said, a sulky expression on his face. "She's not our responsibility anymore, not since she ran off from us."

"But somehow I am sure she is of gentle birth," the marquess reminded him. "And it was all your fault she was abducted. Really, cuz—I am ashamed of you that you are so careless."

Alastair flushed. "I'd like to see the man who would dare attempt anything with that hellion," he muttered, caressing his still bruised jaw. "Besides, I'm not expected at my rooms, and I've no gear with me that's fit for town."

"Stay with me, then, and send for it," the marquess told him.

Alastair sighed to himself. He saw there was no getting out of it, not when Laurence took that tone of voice. As the carriage journeyed toward London, he began to consider his problem. Where was Louisa now? he wondered. Had he lost his last chance to stop her before she began to make mischief? He gnawed a thumbnail, deep in thought. Perhaps he would find her in town? It appeared that was her destination.

He felt a chill creep up his spine when he considered why she was making for the capital, but when he saw his cousin regarding him gravely, he began to talk at great length of a prizefight he had recently seen. The marquess allowed him the diversion, although he had every intention of getting to the bottom of this mess just as soon as he could. That it was a mess, he had no doubt at all.

They arrived at the marquess's town house in Mayfair at dusk. Laurence Russell said nothing until they had eaten a hastily prepared dinner and were enjoying their port alone. Pouring his cousin another glass, he said, "And now I think it time to finish this bout with the gloves off, Alastair. Tell me of this Mrs. Bellings, and why it is so important that you find her—and at once, do you hear?"

Alastair Pettibone looked away after one quick glance at the marquess's face. Then he shrugged and pretended fascination with the wine in the glass before him. "You know, Laurence, that terrible head-of-the-family stare you assume in moments like this is enough to put anyone off," he said as lightly as he could. "And coming the graybeard with me is ludicrous when one considers you are but a few years older.

"As to Louisa Bellings, I beg you not to disturb yourself. I can handle the matter myself. She is no one of importance."

"Then why did you seek her so assiduously? Even sent your grooms to kidnap her?" his cousin persisted.

Alastair shrugged. "The usual, of course. She has some . . . er . . . some rather indiscreet letters I wrote to her, and I wanted them back."

"You were lovers?"

"Yes, since September. It was an enjoyable affair—while it lasted. But, as all such things do, it ceased to amuse me some weeks ago. Since I left her, she has been threatening me, and I do not like to be threatened."

"No one does," Laurence Russell said calmly. "Exactly how indiscreet were you in those letters? Did you propose marriage?"

For the first time Alastair stared at him directly. "Of course not! Think you I have no better care for my name, and yours? Still, as I recall, there were a few phrases that might—just possibly might, you understand—lead those unaware of the situation to consider that marriage was intended."

"Don't tell me, let me guess. You wrote you adored her and always would, am I correct? Perhaps you even told her you could not live without her, and looked forward to spending the rest of your life with her, or somesuch? Alastair, Alastair! Haven't you learned yet that with demimondes, discreetness is everything? Ah, she *is* a demimonde, is she not? She understood the rules of the game? Never tell me you have ruined some bourgeoise innocent!"

"Innocent?" Alastair snorted. "How laughable! She's your age if she's a day, and she's been on the town forever. And if there ever was a Mr. Bellings, he has long since disappeared. Yet she posed as a respectable widow, the soul of gentility, and she is educated and astute. Why she speaks as well as you or I do!"

"A highly unusual woman, or perhaps only an excellent actress," the marquess mused.

"Strange, though, that she would count so much on a few passionate scribbles, if she is, as you say, sagacious. Are you sure you have told me everything?"

He stared hard at his cousin's flushed profile. Lord knows he had had trouble with Alastair Pettibone before, for the man was far from discreet, especially when he knew something others did not. Was it his desire to shine before the ton that made it so hard for him to hold his tongue when given a warm piece of gossip in confidence? Still, as far as the marquess knew, Alastair had never wasted secrets on his mistresses.

As he continued to study him, a mulish look came over his cousin's face, and he sighed. He could see he would get nothing further from the man, not now. But he promised himself he would look into the Bellings matter further. There was something about Alastair's supposedly open admission that did not ring true. And certainly a few warm letters to a member of the muslin set could hardly be enough to force a man to matrimony. It was not as if the woman was a ruined virgin, after all. If she tried to make trouble, she would be put swiftly in her place—and laughed away for her presumptions. He wondered she even tried, if she were as astute as Alastair had painted her.

Accepting defeat for now, he changed the subject. His cousin was so relieved, he did not even protest when Laurence began to discuss the mysterious Miss X again.

"I wonder where she is tonight?" he said, staring past the candlelight to the shadows beyond. "One hopes she reached her destination safely."

"How do you intend to discover her name, where she is?" Alastair asked quickly. "Seems to me you've set yourself a difficult if not impossible task."

"Few things are impossible."

"But—but London is so huge! So many people, so many different ways of life!"

"What you say is true, of course. Yet I do not think I shall have much trouble. Consider all we know of our Miss X."

He held up one finger. "First, she is of the gentry. Will you grant me that?"

He paused until his cousin nodded, albeit grudgingly.

"Two, there is her hair. Such a distinctive color, is it not? I doubt there is another woman in London with hair like that." As his cousin opened his mouth to speak, he went on, "Not of the gentry, at any rate. We are not speaking of opera dancers here.

"Now, that eliminates a number of unsuitable people and locations. Three, there is her age. Perhaps she was being brought up to town for the Season, to make her debut at Almacks?"

Alastair's shout of laughter caused the marquess to raise his brows.

"You cannot be serious, Laurence!" he exclaimed when he could speak again. "That *hoyden*? She was a mere child, and besides, even the fondest of relatives must know she would never take. That horrid hair, her nonexistent manners, her strange behavior. No, no. Surely you are mistaken."

The marquess said nothing for a moment, then he smiled. "Shall we see who has the right of it?" he asked. "Do you care to wager? I say I can have the young lady's name, and her address as well, in less than a fortnight's time."

Alastair grinned. "Done!" he said eagerly. "Nothing I like better than a sure thing! What do you bet?"

"Oh, let us say a hundred guineas—unless that is too shabby for you," Laurence Russell said, a small smile playing over his lips.

"You're on. One hundred guineas it shall be."

He pushed his glass toward the decanter. "Come, we must drink a toast to the wager. And to my unexpected windfall!"

"My father always told me never to count my bag until the day's shoot was over," the marquess remarked as he filled both glasses. "You would be wise to remember that, cuz."

Alastair Pettibone laughed again, a gleam of amusement brightening his hazel eyes as the two touched glasses.

He was feeling much better. Not only had Laurence accepted his explanation for his search for Louisa Bellings, he had suggested a wager he could not possibly win. There was nothing Alastair liked better than getting a march on another man, and when that man was his own, oh-so-superior cousin, his success, when it came, would be sweet indeed.

Six

THE MARQUESS WON the wager the very next morning, and with no effort on his part. At eleven, his butler brought in the Duke of Longford's card and a request for a few minutes of his time. Since Alastair Pettibone was not yet belowstairs, he was permitted a short interval more of blissful ignorance before learning he had lost a hundred guineas. And when he found out his kidnapping victim was none other than the Duke of Longford's niece, he paled, considering what might have happened to him if his cousin had not come to his assistance. But rather than being grateful, Pettibone resented that help. So all-knowing, so unfailing, so—so invincible, the marquess!

Laurence Russell received the duke in the library. He knew William Shaw, of course, for the man had been a friend of his father's, but he had not seen much of him of late. As he exchanged bows with the duke, he studied him carefully. Tall and still slim, with stunning white hair and brows, the duke made an imposing figure. His face in repose was almost austere, but Russell could see the twinkle lurking deep in his eyes.

"But how may I serve you, sir?" he asked, after he had begged the duke to be seated and poured them both a glass of canary.

"I believe you already have," William Shaw said, nodding his approval of the wine.

At the marquess's inquiring look, he explained, "I understand from my niece that you were instrumental in seeing to her reputation and comfort these past two days. At least you did until she ran off from you at dawn yesterday. I have no doubt you would have brought her safely to me in London, but the child was determined to come by herself. You see, she thought to protect the family name by not disclosing it. The young are so often imbued with noble misconceptions, are they not?"

"How did she finally get to town?" the marquess could not stop himself from asking.

"Perched on a load of firewood in the back of a farmer's cart," came the prompt reply.

Laurence Russell choked a little on his wine. "In that scarlet cloak?" he asked when he could speak again. "Good lord, she must have made a picture!"

"She assured me no one saw her but the vulgar, for she did not arrive until late last evening. And she said she had the hood pulled up to conceal her face and hair. I shall have to see if she was right, but I suspect, knowing her, that she will escape this little contretemps—as she has so many in the past."

"She is . . . er . . . prone to getting into scrapes, sir?"

The duke nodded. "You might put it that way, you might indeed. I do not know how it happens, for she does not precisely seek trouble. Trouble, however, seems to find her out with no difficulty at all. But she is very capable of extricating herself from whatever unpleasant situation she finds herself in. I have often marveled at her ability to do this, but then, Penny is not your usual young miss."

"Penny, Your Grace?"

"Ah, yes. She is Miss Penelope Shaw, a daughter of my youngest brother Philip. Since her parents' untimely demise, she has been raised by my sister Eliza in Northumberland."

"And has she come to town to make her bow to society?" Thornbury asked, with an eye to making his prediction come true.

The duke permitted himself a wintry chuckle. "Hardly. Penny does not believe in such things. She considers it degrading. Why, she told me once that the whole business reminded her of a farmer's wife showing off a plump hen on market day, and bragging about how many eggs it could lay."

He ignored the marquess's choked laughter and added, "Of course, she is only seventeen. No doubt she will change her mind one of these days.

"No, it is her older sister who is to come out this spring. Phillipa is as different from Penny as night from day. A lovely blond widgeon, timid as a doe, and with just about as much conversation. She is prone to hysterics and swoons."

"Different, indeed," Thornbury murmured, determined to avoid the other Miss Shaw like the plague. "Miss Penelope showed the utmost courage in the situation she found herself in so inadvertently. But may I explain before I beg your pardon?"

At the duke's nod, he continued, "She would not tell either my cousin or me anything. But somehow she must have picked up a Louisa Bellings's cloak early in the morning two days ago. My cousin is Alastair Pettibone. He had had his grooms out searching for this Mrs. Bellings, and when they spotted your niece wearing that distinctive cloak, they kidnapped her. I do apologize most humbly for my cousin, Your Grace. It was a buffleheaded thing to do, but I gather this Mrs. Bellings is intent on making mischief for him. Some incriminating letters, you understand."

"He is young, too, your cousin?" the duke inquired, his voice sympathetic.

Laurence Russell frowned. "Not young enough to excuse this," he said bluntly. "Alastair is all of twenty-four, and surely that is old enough to know better.

"Heads of households have a great deal to contend with, don't they, sir? I am finding it so more and more."

"Yes, you are right. And it does not get any better as time goes by. But perhaps that is the price we pay for our titles," the duke said as he rose.

His host was quick to get to his feet. "Will you tell your niece that you have called on me, sir?" he could not help asking.

Longford considered for a moment before he shook his head. "No, I don't believe I shall. I'll let her bask in her smug assumption that she saved the family name for a bit. Then, should you chance to meet somehow, as I am sure you will, I shall explain that all her sacrifice was for nothing. Poor girl! She is not used to town ways, and has no idea how small and tight a circle makes up the nobility."

As the two strolled to the door, the marquess said, "May I be so bold as to suggest you keep a close eye on the young lady, sir? Having expanded her horizons from the depths of Northumberland gives endless possibilities for trouble in town. And if Miss Shaw is as you say, trouble is sure to follow."

The duke sighed, but Russell saw his little grin, hastily hidden. "I know," he said simply. "No doubt it is very bad of me, but I have to admit I haven't looked forward so much to a Season in years! Give you good day, sir, and my thanks again.

"Oh, by the way," he added, turning slightly to give the marquess a searching look, "you have a great look of your father. He was an outstanding man, and I see you follow close in his footsteps. He would be proud of you."

Laurence Russell was speechless at the compliment, but he managed to bow the duke away with his usual aplomb.

When his guest was gone, he wandered back to throw himself into a chair by the fireplace. A small blaze there took the chill from the April morning, and for a while, he sat staring into it, chin in hand. Penelope . . . no, Penny Shaw, he told himself. He must be sure to keep an eye on her as well this spring, although he admitted that was no hardship. Like the duke, he was positively looking forward to it—and the difficulties he was sure she would get into. Perhaps he might even be able to rescue her from one or two? It would be his pleasure, for something in him greatly admired her, with her courage, those steady, guileless dark blue eyes, even her mop of flaming curls.

Then he smiled to himself. Miss Shaw might not be ready for London society, but he was equally sure society was not ready for her. He wondered if it ever would be.

Deirdre, Viscountess Manning and the future Duchess of Longford, made an appearance at the duke's town house in Berkeley Square shortly after nuncheon in response to her father-in-law's early morning summons. He saw her alone in a small salon and explained his problem. To his delight, she accepted the charge with great good humor, and he thanked her for it.

"Pooh, sir. It is nothing," she said, tossing her black curls. "And as Robert would tell you, there isn't anything I like better than fashions and shopping. I am sure I shall enjoy both your nieces, and it will cheer me up to take them about. And there is no need to explain Lady Eliza's unsuitability to do so to me. If you recall, I have seen that lady on several occasions. In fact, I doubt I shall ever forget her saying to me on my wedding day that she hoped I would make a frugal manager for Robert, although she doubted that would ever be so, for the amount spent on my gown and our wedding breakfast was not only prodigious but unnecessary! I thought my mama would have a spasm then and there!"

The duke studied his daughter-in-law as she laughed heartily. Deirdre Shaw was a pretty woman of twenty-nine, with a sunny disposition and a merry, contagious laugh that made you smile whenever you heard it. Besides her prompt production of the heir and two other young sons, all of them still in the nursery, he liked her for herself. Indeed, he was sorry that she had miscarried her latest child, and he had hoped taking the girls about would help her to forget that sad event. William Shaw had often told his son how fortunate he was in his wife, something his heir had agreed to with fervor. Would that all marriages were so happy!

He put these reflections aside as Deirdre began to question him about the amount of money she could spend outfitting the girls. When she learned the sum, she looked astounded.

"Yes, Philip left them wealthy indeed. And since Lizzy has spent so little on them all these years they have been growing up, there is plenty more. I want them to have the best.

"Mind you, Deirdre, there may be one small problem," he added. "You see, Penny does not intend to enter society, and so might argue she needs nothing out of the ordinary. You must convince her she is wrong. I have a suspicion that she'll go off faster than her sister, but you shall be the judge. Penny is . . . er . . . a bit of an original."

He then proceeded to tell her, in confidence, of course, of Penny's latest escapade. By the time he reached his niece's unorthodox arrival in Berkeley Square, his daughter-in-law was laughing so hard that the tears ran down her cheeks.

"No more, sir, I beg you!" she gasped. "How—how

ingenious of her! Why, one can only admire such courage! I am anxious to make her acquaintance."

"Yes, but understand I did not tell you about it to amuse you. Rather, I want you to be on your guard."

Lady Manning stopped wiping her eyes on her handkerchief to stare at him. "Think you she will get into some mischief, sir?" she asked.

He nodded vigorously. "There can be no doubt about that! Oh, she will not *mean* to, you understand, but somehow it will happen. You must not be concerned that she will shame us, or behave badly, however. She has good manners, when she remembers to use them. But do, I pray, do your utmost to break her of speaking cant. I can only assume she spent most of her girlhood in the stables.

"Now, as for my other niece . . ."

He grimaced a little, then went on, "Phillipa is your quiet sort, so quiet she can hardly bring herself to speak. I doubt we will fire her off this Season, perhaps any Season, she is so shy. And she is nervous, sensitive, too, from what Lizzy says. I think Lizzy pampers the child too much, even encourages her to swoon and have hysterics when things do not go her way."

His daughter-in-law looked pensive. "Perhaps I am taking on a more onerous chore than I thought?" she mused as if to herself. "Madcaps and megrims, dear, dear!"

The duke leaned forward and took her hand. "Deirdre, I would not ask this of you if I thought there was any possibility of burdening you. You need not live in the girls' pockets. Lizzy and I can squire them to teas and parties, you know."

He looked so worried that Deirdre had to smile. "I promise to tell you if they get too much for me, dear sir. But come, may I meet them now? We could start shopping this afternoon."

In a very few minutes, she saw that the duke had

been speaking only the truth when he described his nieces. Phillipa, after murmuring a faint "so pleased" when they were introduced, sat with her eyes downcast, almost as if she were afraid to look at the visitor. Deirdre tried to put her at her ease, but to no avail. She wondered how the girl intended to go on in company, most especially in gentlemen's company, and inwardly she shuddered.

But she warmed to Penelope in only a minute. The girl had a charming smile, a ready wit, and an enthusiasm that was contagious. The hair was unfortunate, of course, at a time when very pale blondes were admired, but Deirdre thought it like a banner proclaiming Penny Shaw's spirit.

"How kind of you to take us shopping, Lady Manning!" Penny exclaimed when the expedition was proposed. "We have so little idea of what would be suitable for Phil."

"And for you, surely?" Deirdre asked. "I understand you do not care to come out this Season. But even if you do not, you must have walking dresses, morning gowns, at least one or two evening ensembles. There will be many times you will be in company, and you would not care to shame your uncle, now would you?"

"Why, no, of course not," Penny said, a little frown between her brows.

"And certainly your sister will depend on your support," her cousin went on smoothly. "I am sure she will be much more comfortable with you beside her, isn't that so, Miss Shaw?"

Phillipa nodded her head slightly and blushed, and Deirdre hid a sigh. Already she was itching to shake the girl, but she told herself she must have patience, be content with gaining her trust slowly.

Lady Eliza sat somewhat apart, a disgruntled expression on her face. She had had a stormy session with her brother early that morning, and she was feeling very much left out. To think William had forbidden her to go with her nieces. She, who had had the care of them all these years! To think he would trust that goosecap of a young thing to see to everything! Aye, and spend a fortune doing so, too! Just looking at her smart afternoon gown of green faille, her delicate kid gloves, and her plumed hat with its high crown made her feel quite ill. So much money spent on one ensemble! It was a disgrace!

She cleared her throat, and Lady Manning looked at her inquiringly.

"There is no need to run wild, however, Lady Manning," she said in a constricted voice. "One or two simple dresses are all that is required, surely? It is not the thing for young girls to be ostentatious, or to spend a fortune on themselves. Why, it would quite put the gentlemen off I should think, if they were looking for a wife who can manage things with an eye to expenses!"

"I do assure you, dear ma'am, that gentlemen do not consider such matters," Deirdre Shaw said earnestly. "No doubt some of them are quite surprised after marriage to discover how costly a wife can be, but before that happy time, they only enjoy her finery. And it would not do to be seen too often in the same gown. No, no! That would never do! People would talk.

"But come, girls. Shall we begin at once? I know the best modiste in Bond Street. She will be delighted to have the dressing of you. And then there are sandals and gloves and reticules and stoles and . . ."

"You must excuse me," Lady Eliza said as she rose and tottered to the door. "I am feeling quite faint."

Phillipa would have run after her to care for her, except her sister held her tight by the arm. "No, you don't, Phil!" she said firmly. "Aunt will do very well with a maid in attendance. And we have important things to do today. Let us fetch our bonnets at once."

When they met Deirdre in the front hall moments later, that lady tried not to grimace. The loss of her gray cloak forced Penny to wear a warm wool shawl. It was an indeterminate shade of brown, and while it did not clash with her red-gold curls, it could not be said to flatter her. Phillipa's cloak was blue and of a style that had gone out six years before. Deirdre Shaw only hoped Madame would have something more suitable made up for both of them, and she hurried them into her carriage before anyone could come along and see them and wonder who her companions were.

Phillipa was completely cowed, and even Penny, awed, by the grand dressmaking establishment Lady Manning patronized. And they were no less awed by Madame herself, a full-figured woman dressed in smart black taffeta. In fact, Penny whispered when that lady sailed away to fetch her fabrics and patterns, she had been sure Madame was a duchess, if not a royal princess, she held herself so proudly.

Deirdre laughed at her, and assured her Madame Clotilde was a dear behind her gruff exterior—and that the clothes she would provide would be in the height of fashion.

Madame suggested white and palest pink for Phillipa, and a delicate blue-sprigged muslin for morning that had the girl sighing in delight. For evening, several silks in pastel shades with lace and ribbon trimming were bespoke.

"And now my other cousin, Miss Penelope, is also in need of clothes," Lady Manning told the dressmaker.

Madame looked Penny up and down with a critical eye. "She will be a challenge," she said at last. "The pastels suitable for a girl her age would do nothing for her vibrant coloring. What a shame she is not older! I have the most delicious navy satin, but alas, that would never do. However, a biscuit muslin would be attractive with cream lace, and perhaps a jonquil silk? And of course a blue to compliment her eyes, for more formal evenings."

"Perhaps the navy satin would be suitable for an evening cloak?" Deirdre suggested.

Madame clapped her hands. "Superb, m'lady! Your taste is excellent. I shall line it with celestial blue."

"We will also need a cloak or pelisse for daytime. My cousin lost hers on the way to town."

Madame eyed the shawl—and the cloak Phillipa was wearing—and nobly did not shudder. "I shall have to see what I have made up," she said. "Mrs. Jackson returned a cloak last week." She sniffed. "Her husband cut up sharp over her latest bill. Men!" she said scornfully as she went away again.

"Oh, Lady Manning, this will be so expensive!" Penny whispered as soon as Madame was out of earshot. "Aunt Eliza will make us send everything back, too!"

"No, she won't—for she will know nothing of it," Deirdre said earnestly. "The bills are to go directly to your uncle. And that reminds me. I must also order some gowns for your aunt."

She then proceeded to untie a parcel she had brought with her and shake out the wrinkled gown it contained.

"Why, that's aunt's old work gown!" Phillipa said, so startled by the sight of it, it made her forget her shyness.

Lady Manning smiled at her. "She won't need it at the duke's house, surely? I had a maid fetch it for me, for we cannot have your aunt taking you about in dowdy, faded clothes. We must choose some new ones—a gift from her brother so she cannot protest. And you must help me, my dears—tell me what colors she favors, and what styles."

The afternoon was well advanced before they left the dressmaker's, bowed away by Madame Clotilde, who was so pleased with the large commission, she unbent enough to smile. With them, they carried samples of the fabrics they had chosen, so they could match them with sandals and bonnets and stoles.

Only Penny seemed a little absentminded. She was thinking of the habit she had ordered, to be made of a royal blue almost exactly the color of her eyes. How fine she would look in it! she thought, ignoring her smart new cashmere pelisse completely. Now if only Uncle William has a horse I can borrow!

"We shall have to continue our shopping tomorrow, girls," Lady Manning was saying in regret, and Penny made herself forget the habit. "I must return home now, for my babies will be waiting for me."

"Oh, do you have *babies?*" Phillipa asked, her eyes alight. "How old are they?"

If Deirdre was astounded to hear the girl volunteer this speech, she did not show it, and for the ride home regaled the girls with an account of her three sons: Matthew, the five-year-old heir; George, who was three; and James, who had a mere year and a half in his dish.

"I hope we may see them someday soon," Phillipa said as the carriage reached her uncle's town house. "I do so dote on babies."

Deirdre assured her a visit would be arranged, although she noticed that Penny Shaw had shown little interest in the children. Secretly she chuckled. She had been just such a one herself, till motherhood pointed out the error of her ways.

A time was set to meet the following morning, and, refusing their thanks, Lady Manning was driven away.

As the two sisters waited for Tuttle to open the door to their knock, Phillipa whispered, "I pray the duke will not be angry with us, Penny. We have spent so much money! And we are to spend more to-morrow! I know aunt would not approve."

"Aunt is a mean old bit," Penny said shortly, and her sister paled and gasped at her audacity.

Perhaps it was fortunate Tuttle bowed them inside then, before she could say anything further to shock her timid sister.

For the rest of the week, most of the girls' time was spent in Lady Manning's company. Penny soon wearied of the endless shopping and longed for the freedom she had been accustomed to in Northumberland. Here, she was not allowed to step out of the house without a maid, or preferably a sturdy footman, in attendance.

She even found herself getting homesick, something she had never imagined. But oh, how she longed for an early morning gallop in the crisp air, a long hike across the moors, a rainy afternoon curled up with a book from her father's library while Aunt Eliza and Phillipa sat sewing and chatting of household matters. Penny had no more interest in domesticity than she had in infants.

Deirdre Shaw noticed her little downcast look one morning when the girls came to call. Phillipa had excused herself almost at once, to hurry up to the nursery to see the little boys, of whom she had become so fond.

"What is wrong, Penny?" her hostess asked bluntly. "No, no. Do not deny it. I can tell something is bothering you."

Penny tried to smile. "No doubt it is very ungrateful of me, ma'am, but I cannot like town. I never have a moment to myself. Phillipa has become my shadow here, she is so frightened, and my aunt goes on and on at me until I want to put back my head and howl like a dog!"

Deirdre choked a little. "Yes, I have noticed how Phillipa clings to you," she said pensively, when she could speak. "But have you ever considered that might be your fault, my dear?"

"Mine?" Penny asked, her eyes wide with astonishment.

Deirdre nodded. "Do consider," she said. "You have much the stronger personality, and so you take charge of everything—and your sister never has to make a single decision of her own. And if it is not you telling her what to do, it is her aunt. No wonder the child is so timid."

Penny was frowning now. "Yes," she said slowly. "I see what you mean. I have never meant to order her about, you know, it is just that she has always been so dependent on me . . ."

"Oh, she is quite comfortable in that role. But if she does not learn to converse, smile, even flirt, she will have a miserable time of it this spring. What will she do at a party?"

"I have been worried about that, ma'am," Penny admitted. "But what can I do about it?"

"Stand back from her a little. Insist she decide things for herself. Ask her opinion, include her in table conversation. Tell her you will not be her shield and buckler anymore," Deirdre said briskly. "We do not have much time. The duke is planning a ball for Phillipa, and before that there will be endless invitations. Phillipa *must* be more forthcoming."

"I will do what I can," Penny said glumly. "Perhaps all will be well. Phil is so sweet and lovely, is she not? Perhaps there will be one gentleman who will not care she has no conversation."

Or wit, or liveliness, Deirdre thought, mentally shaking her head. She knew she should be thinking it a shame that all those attributes had been given to Penny Shaw in such abundance, instead of being divided equally between the sisters, but she had become so fond of the younger girl, she would not have had her change one iota.

Seven

THE PLAIN-FACED, MIDDLE-AGED maid who answered Louisa Bellings's discreet knock the same day Penny arrived in London, smiled broadly when she saw who stood on the step.

"Miz Louisa!" she exclaimed, reaching for the portmanteau the visitor carried. "Ain't seed ye this age, I ain't! Come in, come in, do! Miz April be that glad ter see ye, too, she will."

She grimaced as she shut the door. " 'Least she will when she finds out 'bout it," she said, lowering her voice.

Both women looked up the stairway that rose on the left side of the small front hall.

"April has company, Nan?" Louisa Bellings asked as she removed her stole and bonnet and handed them to the maid. "I understand. I'll just wait in the kitchen till she's free."

As the maid led the way down the hall, lugging Louisa's case, she said over her shoulder, "Pretty reg'lar company 'e is, too. Comes 'ere two nights outta three, an' sometimes afternoons as well. Course 'e's a new one. Miz April's only been in 'is keepin' fer a month."

"I thought the house looked quite well. Had it painted, did she?"

"Nah, 'e did. Brings 'er all kinds o' presents, too, though both o' us wish that stupid canary would

87

die. She never takes the cover off 'cept when 'e's 'ere. Cuppa, Miz Louisa?"

The visitor nodded as she took a seat at the wooden table in the center of the kitchen. The maid swung the kettle over the fire and set out the teapot, two cups and saucers, and a plate of biscuits. As she worked, she said, "Don't know why 'tis men are so foolish! As if Miz April needed a canary! Much better ter give 'er jewels or money, is wot I say."

"I'm sure he does that, too," Louisa said as she smoothed her hair. "April's always looked after the main chance."

Nan chuckled and nodded her head. "Ye been outta town, Miz Louisa?" she asked as she filled the teapot with boiling water to warm it. "Ain't seed ye about, like."

"Yes, out of town. But I had to come back for something very important. Tell me, Nan—is Blackie still in business?"

The maid peered at her. "Wot would ye want wit' the likes o' 'im?" she asked. Then she shook her head. "Not that ye'll tell me. Keep a deal ter yerself, an' always 'ave done.

"Yeah, 'e's still around. Law ain't caught up wit' 'im yet."

"You sound sorry it is so," Louisa said, her brows raised. "What's Blackie ever done to you, that you would wish him bad luck?"

The maid set her mouth in a thin line and looked stubborn, and Louisa Bellings clasped her hands before her on the table. In the front of the house, she could hear a canary trilling an endless song. It made a cheerful noise, although she quite agreed it would be enough to send you to Bedlam if you had to listen to it for very long.

The two sat over the teacups for some time, exchanging gossip and reminiscing about old friends. Nan did not notice how one-sided a conversation was, for Louisa Bellings was skillful at asking leading questions—and seldom volunteered any information of her own.

When the front door slammed, they both heard it, and only a few minutes later, a pretty little blonde came into the kitchen, tying the sash of a violet silk wrapper. She shrieked when she saw the visitor sitting there, and rushed to give her a kiss and a big hug.

"Louisa! My word, what a surprise! Have you been waiting for me long? Come into the parlor, do," the blonde named April invited, without waiting for an answer. "Nan, bring the sherry.

"Just let me shut this damned bird up," she muttered as they entered the front room. "Drives me mad!" she added as she twitched a cover over the cage. The canary stopped abruptly in mid trill.

"There now, that's better," April said as she collapsed on the sofa and arranged a pile of silk pillows behind her head. "Take that chair, dearie. It's the most comfortable.

"Now, what brings you here? I thought you buried in the midlands."

"I was, but circumstances made it imperative for me to return to town. The problem is, April, I've no place to stay . . . and I'm hoping you'll put me up."

Louisa seemed to see the little reluctance on her friend's face, for she hastened to add, "I can pay, don't worry. The thing is, I let my rooms go two months past, not that I could go back there in any case."

"You in trouble, Louisa?" April asked, eyeing her shrewdly.

Her visitor nodded shortly, but before she could say more, Nan brought in the sherry and the glasses.

"That will do," her mistress said. "Shut the door when you leave, Nan."

The maid pouted a little at being left out, but did as she was told.

"What kind of trouble?" April asked, just as if they had not been interrupted at all.

"Nothing serious, believe me. I've lost something. It means a lot of money to me, and I intend to get it back. And I'm not exaggerating. A *lot* of money. And if you'll help me, I'll see you get a share. There'll be plenty, you'll see."

"What's your lay? Indiscreet letters? Pregnancy?"

"No, nothing so ordinary. Much, much better, and much more profitable."

"Don't know about that. You remember that colonel in the Guards? Squeezed him good, I did, when I threatened to go to his mother about us. His *mother*, mind you!"

Louisa smiled, looking amused.

"Well, what's it all about, then?" April asked before she took a healthy swig of her sherry.

"That I can't say. It's too dangerous. And what you don't know can't hurt you. There's risk here, you see.

"But I need a place where I can stay for a couple of weeks. And I promise I won't be any trouble."

"There'll be none, as long as m'lord don't catch sight of you. He's a nervous one. Had to work twice as hard on him after he heard the door knocker. Finally had to tell him it was only a gown I'd ordered being delivered before he'd relax again."

"We'll have some sort of signal, then. If I'm out and he comes, pull one of the curtains at your window aside. I'll stay away until after he goes."

When April nodded, she changed the subject to ask about some of the other demimondes they both knew. April spent a happy hour describing this one and that's downfall, or lack of protectors, or just plain bad luck.

"The only one doin' well, 'sides me, is that damned

Harriet Wilson," she said at last. Her voice had thickened a little as the level of the sherry in the decanter sank. "Saucy tart, she is. An' now she's in the keepin' o' a great man, she 'ardly speaks ter me. Ridin' fer a fall, she is."

"Nan tells me Blackie's still about. How do I get in touch with him?" Louisa asked, abruptly changing the subject.

"Lor, Blackie?" April asked, her china blue eyes wide. "Ask Nan, she'll know. Sweet on 'im, she was, at one time, an' she keeps track o' 'im. But I won't 'ave 'im 'ere, Louisa! Ye'll 'ave ter meet 'im somewheres else, ye ken?"

Lousia nodded as she rose to straighten her crushed skirts.

"Lor, look at ye!" April jeered. "Jess like a Puritan ye be in that nasty gray gown. Gives me the megrims, it do."

"I'll have you know I've been posing as a respectable married lady," Louisa told her. "I think I'll go and unpack my things, if you'll show me where I'm to sleep. And I'll pay you now for the first week. Same as I charged you when you needed a place, all right?"

Her hostess nodded, and she handed over a small pile of coins. "Come on, get up now. And you'd better have a nap. At our age we have to be careful of our looks, you know."

April jeered at her as she hauled herself up from the sofa's embrace and led the way upstairs. But behind her, Louisa Bellings was silently shaking her head. April had gone downhill in only the few months she'd been away. It wouldn't be long now before she wouldn't be able to attract a wealthy lord, afford a little house like this one, not long before she'd be on the streets with all the other drabs. Trouble with April was, she didn't think ahead, make plans to insure her future, as I have, Louisa thought as she inspected the tiny room at the back of the house that was to be hers. Well, better her than me.

Later, after she had changed to a tawdry old gown, arranged her hair quite differently, and wrapped herself in a ragged, enveloping shawl she borrowed from Nan, she left the house for the tavern where the maid had told her Blackie could be found in the early evenings. She walked quickly, impatient to set her schemes in motion, and determined not to fail.

A hungry old man sidling up to her to beg a penny, took one look at the dark anger on her hard face and shrank back into a doorway without saying a word.

The tavern, when she found it, was no better and no worse than many others like it in this poor part of town. Patronized by the dregs of London's underground, it was filled with drinkers of both sexes. Louisa elbowed her way up to the scarred table that served as a bar and ordered a half-pint of knock-me-down, a popular heavy beer. Only a glance around the smoke-filled room told her Blackie was not there. No matter, she thought as she made for a stool just being vacated. She'd wait.

It was almost an hour later before the man she sought made an appearance, trailed by two of his henchmen. The tavern quieted for a moment when he swaggered in, then everyone began to talk again, carefully ignoring the huge man whose head almost touched the low rafters of the ceiling.

Louisa saw him snap his fingers at a table of men. They quickly vacated it, and she rose to go to him.

"Get away wit' ye!" one of his henchmen said in a shrill voice when he saw what she was about. "Blackie don't want nuffin' ter do wit' the likes of ye!"

"I am sure you are wrong," Louisa said calmly as she took a seat. "Hello, Blackie. Haven't seen you this age."

"Why, stab me dead if it ain't Louisa Bellings!" the big man crowed, grabbing her chin and giving her a hearty, wet kiss. "Wot ye want then?"

"How can you be so sure I want anything?" she countered, stifling the urge to wipe her mouth on her sleeve.

He roared with laughter. "Ye wouldn't be 'ere, else, now would ye? Always thought yerself too good fer the likes o' me."

She tried a smile. "Very well. I see I must confess. But I'd speak to you privately."

"Get us both a pint o' knock-me-down, then make yerselves scarce," he growled over his shoulder. His two men hurried away.

"I've a proposition for you," Louisa Bellings said after their beer had been delivered and they were alone again. "A job, if you like. It's worth a great deal of money . . ."

"How much?" he demanded before he swallowed half his pint.

She named a sum that made him narrow his eyes and whistle softly. "Ye mean it?" he asked, watching her face carefully.

She nodded. "Are you interested?" she asked.

"Int'rested? 'Course I am. Fer that I'd murder the lord mayor!"

"It won't come to murder. At least I don't think it will. Now, here is what happened, and what I propose to do . . ."

The two edged their chairs closer together, and Louisa began to whisper in his ear.

Penny was quick to tell her uncle at dinner one evening that her new habit had arrived—and how she hoped to be able to ride in the park. The duke, who had noticed how bored she was becoming with all the shopping, agreed at once. Keep her busy, he told himself. That way there'll be less chance of her getting into trouble.

"I'll look in at Tattersall's for a neat mare for you, m'dear," he said.

"I should love to go with you," Penny replied, her eyes shining.

Longford shook his head, looking suddenly severe. "That you will not do, my girl. Females are never seen at Tattersall's."

"Whyever not?" Penny demanded, while her aunt Eliza made disapproving noises from the other end of the table, and Phillipa put down her fork in trepidation, her appetite quite gone.

"Because they aren't," the duke said brusquely. "And you will not be the first to break tradition, is that quite clear?"

"Oh, well, if it is a request from you, sir, certainly not," she said, with a sunny smile. "Still, I do think it rather ridiculous. After all, surely a woman knows better what would suit her when it comes to choosing a mount. And women are as smart as men."

"Much as it desolates me to contradict you, my dear Penny, you are wrong," Longford said, cutting his veal. "It is a well-known fact that men are the more intelligent of the species, no doubt about it."

"Of course that silly theory was advanced by men," she said. "How typical!"

"Penelope!" Lady Eliza said in an awful voice. "Not another word from you! Such sass, and to the duke, too!"

"I keep forgetting his august rank," Penny admitted as she buttered a roll. "To me he is simply my dear uncle."

"Trying to turn me up sweet, are you?" that gentleman demanded, bending toward her slightly and looking affronted.

Penny chuckled. "Now how could I ever do that,

when as one of the superior male sex, you would find me out in a moment? Don't you agree with me, Phil—that such a thing would be impossible?"

Since Phillipa was tongue-tied, it was just as well the duke's laughter—and the way he shook his finger at his saucy niece—saved her from any reply.

Later, as their plates were being removed, the duke turned to Phillipa and said, "But I have been most remiss! Do you care to ride with Penny, Phillipa? If so, I shall provide two mounts."

The girl turned pale and shook her head, and although she looked pleadingly at her sister, Penny refused to answer for her. At last she said in a voice only above a whisper, "Please do not, uncle. I—I am not fond of riding."

"Frightened?" he asked, trying for a kindly tone. When her eyes filled with tears, he patted her hand. "There now, no need to be upset about it. Many ladies do not care to ride for pleasure. But if I am to squire Penny in the park mornings, you must allow me to drive you in the afternoons."

Phillipa could not even smile and nod, and the duke sighed and picked up his wineglass. Penny stared at her sister as if trying to will her to answer, but Phillipa would not look at her.

Frustrated, Penny sighed herself. She had been trying as hard as she could to follow Deirdre's instructions with regards to Phil, but she had to admit it was heavy going. And later, when they left the duke to his port, Phil begged her not to call attention to her, for it upset her so.

"Well, I do not know how you are to go on then," Penny said, more than a little annoyed. "What will you do when a gentleman wishes to converse with you? You must try harder, Phil. And surely this shrinking reluctance you practice is absurd in a family setting!"

Phillipa hung her head. "It is easy for you," she

said in a strangled voice. "You are so sure of yourself. So brave. But I am not like that, nor will I ever be."

She looked up then to see her sister regarding her with a dismayed expression, and added softly, "Uncle William frightens me. He is so fierce!"

"Nonsense," Penny said briskly. "He's an old dear, and if you weren't such a ninny, you'd see that for yourself."

"But I can't tease him like you do," Phillipa said as she began to cry. "I—I should just die if I tried!"

Lady Eliza came in then and demanded to know what Penny had been saying to upset her sister. Taking the older girl into her ample embrace, she glared at Penny over her shoulder. "As I have told you time without number, dear Phillipa is both nervous and sensitive. Special care must be taken of her, you thoughtless girl!"

Penny held her tongue with an effort, but she had no intention of giving up her struggle to make her sister more at ease in company. But as she told Lady Manning the following day, she did not think she had much chance of succeeding. Deirdre begged her to persevere.

Penny's new mare was duly delivered to the duke's stables in the mews. She was all glossy black, except for a white blaze. Penny clapped her hands in delight when she saw her and declared she could not wait to try out her paces. The duke told her they would ride before breakfast the following morning—and took her into the house to lecture her on proper etiquette when in Hyde Park, even at that early hour. Penny listened and nodded, although she was quick to say she thought the ban on galloping too archaic to be believed.

Later that afternoon, as she was leaving a shop on Bond Street, followed by her sister and her cousin, Penny saw the Marquess of Thornbury strolling toward them. Her face paled, and she hurried to reach the safety of the carriage.

The marquess was beside them before she could succeed however, and he greeted Lady Manning as an old friend. As he bowed to her companions, Deirdre said, "Let me make you known to my cousins, Thornbury. This is Miss Phillipa and Miss Penelope Shaw. They are come to town to enjoy the Season. Cousins, Laurence Russell, Marquess of Thornbury."

Penny had been trying to catch Deirdre's eye, so somehow she could warn her that their names must not be given to this handsome peer, but to no avail. Inwardly she groaned at the revelation.

"My pleasure, ladies," he said, with another bow.

"How do you do?" Penny asked, for she knew Phillipa incapable of speech with a stranger. She sounded so stiff that both her companions looked at her, surprised.

At once, Deirdre Shaw came to the rescue, asking the marquess of his family and giving him the news of hers. It seemed a long time before their tête-à-tête was over, for neither Penny nor her sister contributed a word.

Thornbury waved the groom away, so he could assist first Deirdre and then Phillipa into the carriage. As he held out his arm to Penny, he leaned closer to whisper, "So we meet again, 'Miss Smith.' You are looking a great deal better than when I saw you last. And I am so glad you have not cut your hair to be fashionable. It would be a crime if even one blazing curl was missing."

Penny only climbed into the carriage so hurriedly that she gave the marquess and any other interested passerby a very good look at a pair of neat ankles.

As they were driven away, she began to talk of the purchases they had just made, for she had no desire to mention the marquess. But could anything be more unfortunate? she asked herself as they traveled along. She had hoped never to see the man—or his obnoxious cousin—again. And now he knew her name!

Still, she thought as she looked down at her new afternoon gown of gold lutestring with its smart braid trim, she could not help but be a little proud of her appearance. She did not look like some grubby schoolgirl now, and she was glad of it. And perhaps the marquess would keep her adventures getting to town to himself. If she saw him again, she told herself, she would make a point of asking him to. Not that she wanted to see him. Of course not!

But the very next morning, while riding with her uncle in the park, they were hailed by Laurence Russell, coming from the opposite direction on a big chestnut gelding. As he raised his hand, the duke reined in, and Penny was forced to follow suit.

"Your Grace, Miss Shaw," he said as he removed his top hat.

"Well met, Thornbury. So you have met my niece, have you?"

"Yesterday afternoon on Bond Street. Your daughter-in-law introduced us."

"Ah, yes, Deirdre! She has been so helpful, taking the girls about shopping. Do you care to join us, Thornbury? Penny is trying out her new mare."

Obediently the marquess wheeled his horse. As they began to trot, three abreast, he said, "Have you named her yet, ma'am?"

Penny's heart was racing, and she had to take a deep breath before she admitted she had not.

"May I suggest Runaway?" the marquess said in a bland voice.

Penny darted him a pleading look, and he nodded a little before he addressed her uncle.

She barely attended to their conversation, for she was thinking hard. Somehow she had to manage a few moments alone with the marquess, so she could beg his silence with the ton. How she was to do this she did not know, until the duke solved her problem for her neatly, by begging to be excused for a moment when he saw a friend walking nearby.

"Just go ahead. I'll rejoin you in a minute," he said. "Must ask the viscount how his ailing wife is doing."

As his niece and the marquess trotted away, Duke Longford permitted himself a tight little smile.

"I am so glad to have this chance to talk to you alone," Penny said quickly. "I had no idea you knew my uncle!"

"I know most of society. And the duke was a friend of my father's."

"Please, sir, I beg you—do not mention our earlier meeting," Penny said earnestly. "Not to anyone."

"But the duke is aware of it. He came to see me the day after you arrived in London."

"He did? Whatever for?" she asked, sounding stunned.

The marquess shrugged. "He wanted to thank me for taking care of you. And that reminds me, young lady, I must take exception to your running off as you did that morning in Milfield. Have you any idea of the to-do you left behind? The Pettibones were sure you were a thief and had made off with some of the plate. And Elizabeth Pettibone would have it that you had stolen her tarantula. Such carrying on, so many screams of joy when he was discovered safe in his container."

Torn between annoyance that her elaborate scheme to keep the marquess from learning her family name had been both unnecessary and fruitless, and amusement at Russell's story, Penny chose to laugh. "Oh, no. Do not say so! She could not possibly think I had designs on . . . er . . . Algernon!"

"Of course she did!" the marquess said promptly. "Being so intrigued with him herself, she cannot imagine that others might find him repulsive."

"Is he?"

"Decidedly. Huge and hairy and ugly as sin. Made m'skin crawl."

"It makes mine crawl, too, just hearing about him," Penny admitted. Then she turned serious and said, "Will you be able to keep your cousin from blurting out what happened?"

"Alastair will say nothing. The kidnapping hardly reflects well on him, you know, and he would prefer no one learn of it."

Penny drew a deep, relieved breath. "It is not that I mind for myself," she said gruffly. "It is my uncle's and my sister's reputations that concern me. As for what the ton thinks of me, I hardly care."

"Still, may I suggest you do not give society any reason to talk about you? For what you do here in town reflects directly on your relatives. You must be circumspect."

Penny could not like being lectured by this superior gentleman, and when she and her uncle parted company from him later, her farewell was positively frosty. It did nothing for her temper when she noted that both Thornbury and her uncle seemed somewhat amused by her, as if she were nothing more than a precocious child.

Men! she thought as she rode home seething. Men!

Eight

LATER THAT MORNING, Alastair Pettibone took leave of his cousin—with many expressions of gratitude for all his help.

"Assure you, obliged to you for putting me up, cuz," he said as he wiped his mouth on his napkin preparatory to leaving the breakfast room, and his cousin's house. "But my own rooms are ready now, and my valet has brought my clothes to town. No need to inconvenience you any longer."

Thornbury made a noncommittal sound, for in all honesty, he could not say he would miss Alastair. He had never really cared for him, and he disapproved of the company he kept and his useless way of life—the gambling, the drinking, the wenching.

During the week Alastair had been in residence, he had not tried to question him further about this Louisa Bellings he was so anxious to find, but Laurence Russell had not forgotten her. He did not believe for a moment that his cousin was distraught because of a few misguided love letters and possible blackmail, and he intended to pursue the matter. And, he told himself, looking as black as when Penny had first seen him, if he discovered anything, anything at all, that Alastair had been up to that would reflect badly on the family name, he would be quick to act.

"Must also thank you for assisting me with the young Shaw girl," Alastair was saying now, and he forced himself to concentrate. "I would have been in a pretty pass, her uncle being Duke Longford. When I think what might have happened, I shudder. Whew!"

"All's well that ends well, eh?" the marquess asked as he poured another cup of coffee. Then he stared at his cousin. "Remember, Alastair—no one must ever learn of it. No one."

"Of course not!" Alastair blustered as he pushed his chair back and rose to bow. "No doubt I shall see you about this Season. Bid you good day, cuz."

Thornbury did not bother to rise, only waving a careless hand as he picked up his morning post again.

Alastair Pettibone whistled in relief as he strolled away from the mansion in Pall Mall. It had been difficult for him, staying with his cousin, for he sensed the man's disapproval. And it was hard to pretend to like him, be easy with him, when in reality he had a distinct antipathy for the man. It had not been so bad when they were younger, but when Laurence had come into the title, the estates, the fine old London house, and all the wealth due the only son of the former marquess, he had been eaten up with jealousy. He considered his own portion very small for a man of his scope, and he was forever trying to improve it. Unfortunately for him, gambling had so far done little more than bring him to the brink of ruin. Oh, he would have an occasional run of good luck, but all too often the cards fell for his opponents, his horses were unplaced, his cock couldn't be brought up to scratch. What he would do if he could not find Louisa before she began to make mischief, he did not know, and his long, thin face darkened when he considered the consequences. He would be ruined, forced to flee the country. Where he would go now that Europe had been effectively closed to him by Napoléon's

Grande Armee—and relations with the United States were so strained again—he did not know.

He had to find Louisa, he had to! And when he did, he told himself as he turned into King Street, he would not hesitate to do whatever had to be done to silence her once and for all.

He would have been astounded to learn that he was not the only one searching for her, and that at that very moment, his cousin was interviewing a private agent he had engaged to discover the whereabouts of a certain Mrs. Louisa Bellings.

"Sorry I am to report, sir, that I've no news for you, none at all," the agent, a Mr. Samuel Bottoms, said sadly. "But there's a lot of London I've not had the chance to investigate."

"I understand," Thornbury said, trying to hide his impatience. He told himself it would have been folly to expect the woman to fall into his hands like a ripe plum, but still, the delay was worrying. He knew she had been making for London, hot in pursuit of the ladies Shaw, but where was she now? Gone to ground somewhere in this vast city with its warrens of tenements, rooming houses, and hotels? He did not think Alastair had heard from her, either, for he had made it a point to inspect the morning post every day before his cousin came down.

He noticed the agent was shifting uneasily from one large foot to the other, and he dismissed him with another purse for his expenses.

He was still sitting in the library, going over the facts he knew and remembering how brilliant Penny Shaw's red-gold curls had looked in the early morning sunlight, when his butler brought in Bartholomew Whitaker's card.

Thornbury's eyes grew thoughtful. He was a friend of Whitaker's, to be sure, but not one of his intimate circle. What could the man want? Was it something to do with Alastair and his hasty departure from the country?

When the butler showed him in, nothing of his thoughts showed in Thornbury's face. "How do you do," he said, rising to shake hands. "I thought you were visiting Feathers in the country."

"I was. Deadly dull. Invented an excuse to leave, saying my cousin needed me. You remember Jason Howland, don't you?"

"Of course," Thornbury said easily as he waved his guest to a seat. "How is he? Haven't seen him for a while."

"Mending nicely, thank you," Whitaker said as he sat down.

"I was unaware he had been ill."

"Heartbroken, two years ago. But he's recovered at last, for which loud hosannas sound! He's found a darling little opera dancer."

Thornbury smiled. "But why did you have to invent an excuse to leave the country?" he could not help asking. "Thought Feathers was a friend of yours."

"He is. It's his mother. Rules that roost with an iron hand. And you know, Thornbury, at almost twenty-nine, I rather think I can manage my own life without interference."

He mused for a moment and added slowly, "I think it was her ordering me to get out of my wet clothes one afternoon after we got caught in a rain shower while riding that did it. She also told me to towel off well, and insisted I drink a hot posset as a precaution."

As the marquess laughed, he added, "After that, I could hardly wait to be gone. Poor Alan! Man's been living under the cat's paw for so long he doesn't even notice her. But I expect his arrival in town shortly.

"Is your cousin Pettibone here, too?" he asked next.

Thornbury considered him closely, but he could see little but casual interest in the man's face and sleepy, half-closed eyes.

"Yes, we came up together a day after we met you. He's been staying here, but he's gone back to his own rooms now they're ready for him."

"Since I refuse to believe that young thing you were escorting had anything whatsoever to do with you, I must assume she is one of Alastair's interests? I do admit I was surprised that she was with both of you, however."

Thornbury rose and walked to a window that overlooked Pall Mall. When he turned he had his face under firm control. "That young thing is none of your affair, Whitaker," he said, his soft words at odds with the rebuff.

Bartholomew Whitaker shrugged. "Of course she isn't. Only thought it singular, y'know. And I am aware of your cousin and the company he keeps. I've often thought it damned hard on you, Thornbury, Alastair and his escapades."

"No doubt he was put on earth to keep me humble," the marquess said. Whitaker laughed and changed the subject.

It took Louisa Bellings a full week of searching before she found Penny Shaw at last. Every day of that week, dressed once again as a demure widow, she had spent being driven by Blackie in a hansom cab through the streets of Mayfair, looking, always looking. She would have liked to stroll through Hyde Park in the late afternoons when the fashionable world assembled there, to search as well, but she did not dare, for here in London, she was both the huntress and the hunted. She knew Alastair Pettibone must be searching for her just as assiduously as she sought her own quarry, and she had no intention of falling into his hands.

She was beginning to feel a little desperate when Blackie drove her back to April's house after another fruitless day. Why, she told herself, for all I know, the girl may have left London by now. I must find her quickly. I must!

Luck smiled on her the very next morning. The hansom had just entered Berkeley Square from Charles Street when she saw the girl she sought coming down the steps of a mansion across the way. She was accompanied by the delicate blonde Louisa remembered well, and both girls were attended by a sturdy footman. And there was no mistaking the red-gold curls that peeked from beneath Penny Shaw's fashionable bonnet. The two girls were assisted into a handsome town carriage and driven away.

Abruptly telling Blackie to wait for her, Louisa climbed down from the cab and hurried around the square—to stare at the uncommunicative black door with its polished brass knocker as if she could wring the occupant's name from it by sheer force of will. She was about to go away when an elderly lady left the house next door with her maid. Louisa went toward her, a tentative smile on her face.

"I do beg your pardon, ma'am," she said, dropping a curtsy. "I wonder if you would be so kind as to help me?"

The lady stared at her, affronted at being accosted this way by a perfect stranger, but Louisa's demure gray gown and pelisse, her ladylike demeanor, stood her in good stead.

"I thought I spied a dear young friend of mine leaving the house next to yours a few minutes ago," she said when the lady nodded. "I have not seen her for some time, and although I promised to come to her when I arrived in town, I carelessly misplaced her address. Such a silly thing to do, was it not? And so vexing! I hesitated to inquire until I was sure I had not been mistaken."

"That is the Duke of Longford's town house," the elderly lady said. "William Shaw, you know. He has his two young nieces and his sister visiting."

Lousia gave her a heartfelt smile. "Thank you so much, ma'am," she said as she curtsied again. "I shall write to Penny, care of her uncle, and arrange a time to call. You have been most kind."

As she turned back the way she had come, Louisa forced herself not to run in her exultation. At last! she told herself as she reached the cab and winked at Blackie. I have her at last! And now we shall see!

She told Blackie to drive them to the poor tavern he frequented. They had to make plans, careful plans, for Louisa Bellings knew she could not approach the house where Penny Shaw resided and beg admittance. No, not after her anger at losing the scarlet cloak had caused her to abandon her genteel act and scream at the girl's relatives like any Billingsgate wench.

Once they were seated at their usual table, Blackie suggested a break-in, but Louisa dissuaded him.

"The house is sure to be crammed with servants, man! The owner's a duke, no less! And any break-in would have to be done very late at night. Even then, someone might hear. It's too risky."

Blackie scowled across the scarred table at her. "Mayhap yer right," he said grudgingly. "Still an' all, 'twould be the quickest way, see?"

"I wonder if we could bribe one of the servants," Louisa said thoughtfully, staring down into the beer she had yet to taste. "Or get one of your own men engaged there."

Blackie barked a derisive laugh. "Not bloody

likely anyone *I* knows would be 'ired on! But mebbe we could *persuade* someone ter tell us where the cloak is-like? Mebbe even get 'em ter lift it fer us?"

Louisa studied his hard face and hoped he would never have a chance to "persuade" her to anything.

"I do know a 'andsome young feller. I'll set 'im ter flirtin' with the maids, see wot 'e can find out," he said. "There's no 'urry, is there?"

"Nooo . . ." she said slowly. "Not for a while yet. But the sooner the cloak is in my hands, the better. Yes, hire your young fellow. You and I must watch Miss Penny, try to discover her routine, whom she visits, things like that. We may be able to grab her, if luck is with us."

Luck was not with them in this instance, however. Although they certainly learned a great deal about Penny Shaw in only a few days of trailing her, Louisa was quick to see that any kidnapping attempt would be futile. The girl was always accompanied by her sister and sometimes her aunt as well, or a dashing young woman she learned was Deirdre Shaw, Viscountess Manning. But it was not just that her quarry was surrounded by females. Blackie could have made short work of them. No, it was because she was also attended by either a footman or grooms.

Louisa was not too disappointed. She had been feeling uneasy ever since she had learned Penny Shaw had such an exalted relative. And although she had never had any dealings with dukes, she suspected they were much more difficult to hoodwink than other men, and had more resources at their command if they were threatened.

She was frowning a little as she walked once again to the lowly tavern some days later in response to a summons from Blackie. As she came toward him, she saw he looked cheerful enough, for he grinned as he waved her to a stool.

"I think I've found the very wench," he said, with no preamble. "Kitchen maid she is. New ter the 'ouse, an' green. Fell fer Kenny in a thrice, she did. An' she's got an ailin' mother. I 'aven't spoken ter 'er yet, but I'm sure I can make 'er see it our way."

"I don't like using a young girl," Louisa said, frowning.

"Wot? Yer goin' soft on me?" Blackie asked in some astonishment.

"Of course not! But young girls are not as dependable as men. And even if we offer her money, instead of threatening her, she might be too frightened to carry it off."

"She'll do as she's told, or else she won't 'ave a mother ter worry about," Blackie growled, his dark frown making him look as horrid as the evilest pirate had ever done. Louisa saw a man at the next table get up abruptly to leave, and she did not wonder at it.

"Very well," she said as she rose, too, and fastened her old shawl across her bosom. "See what you can do, Blackie. But be careful. Nothing must go wrong."

"Nothin' will," he said, raising his pint in a toast. "Ter riches, Louisa. Ter riches!"

Lady Manning gave a small tea party to introduce her new cousins to her acquaintances. "Of course it is the shabbiest thing," she told them when she extended the invitation. "I should much prefer giving a soiree for you, or a picnic at Richmond, but I suspect Phillipa will be more comfortable with a smaller group composed entirely of ladies at first. Isn't that so, my dear?"

Phillipa just looked frightened.

"Soon, however, you must begin to go to other affairs," the lady went on firmly. "And the duke has already sent invitations to everyone who is anyone in the ton for your ball in May. That reminds me. We must get special gowns for you both. We should see Madame Clotilde as soon as possible, to give her time to concoct something wonderful. My dear father-in-law's entertainments are always out-standing."

Penny saw that Phillipa looked ready to swoon now, and she changed the subject.

The tea party passed without incident, although Phillipa had little to say for herself and could not be persuaded to pass the cups. Penny had to perform that task for her while her sister sat close to her aunt, trying not to cringe when anyone addressed a remark to her. Since Penny had heard one of the older ladies call her sister "a sweet girl, so modest!" she was not too depressed, although she suspected that the size of Phil's dowry and the number of unwed sons the lady had, had something to do with her smiling approval.

Eventually the Shaw girls were invited to evening parties as well, and these occasions were very hard on Phillipa. She *tried*, she told her sister when they returned home late at night, she *did*! But it was so difficult! The men were so sophisticated, were they not? So—so sure of themselves, so—so witty and quick! She could never think of anything to say to them.

And then she would dissolve in tears and have to be helped to bed. The next day invariably saw her remain there with a sick headache.

It was after one of these evenings that Penny decided she must speak to Lady Manning alone. Things could not go on as they were, and she did not know what she could do about it.

"You can see as well as I can, Deirdre, that Phil is not getting any easier in company," she told her as they sat in the privacy of the lady's sitting room. "And what to do with her, I do not know!"

Deirdre smiled a little. "I know how vexing it is for you, my dear Penny. But I had the most marvelous idea last night, just as I was dropping off to sleep. And it might—it just possibly might—work."

"I can't imagine what it could be, short of turning Phil into a completely different girl," Penny said, her expression gloomy.

"Oh, that I were a conjurer!" Lady Manning said, with a chuckle. "But listen, and tell me what you think. I have noticed that Phillipa is only really natural when she is with my children. Would you agree?"

"Yes, you are right about that. She has always adored babies and little children. Perhaps because they do not challenge her, as adults seem to?"

"And wouldn't you also agree that she shows to best advantage with them?" Deirdre persisted. "So happy she is then, so full of smiles and games to play? Even so talkative?"

"Yes, but we cannot take your little boys to evening parties, ma'am," Penny pointed out, looking confused.

Her hostess chuckled again. "What a ghastly picture that conjures up! No, of course we can't. But I think I can provide the perfect setting nevertheless. I have written to a cousin of mine—such a dear, good man he is!—and he has promised to come up to town from his home in Kent— No, I shall say nothing more. It is my little secret. But be ready to bring Phillipa here someday soon when my summons comes. And then we shall see!"

Penny thought her very mysterious, but since she met the Marquess of Thornbury on her way from the front door to her uncle's carriage, all thoughts of Deirdre flew from her mind at once.

"Miss Sm—Shaw," he said as he bowed. "I saw you last evening at the Earl and Countess of Haverford's reception, did I not? But it was such a

111

perfect crush, I was unable to greet you. I am glad to see you going about in society, even though I understand from your uncle, you rather scorn the institution."

"I, m'lord?" Penny asked, her eyes wide and guileless. "You must be mistaken. Not that I would have been there if it had not been for my sister. She depends on my company, you see."

"Do you attend Mrs. Kincaid's soiree in three days' time?" he asked next.

Penny nodded. "Perhaps you would save me a dance," Thornbury persisted.

She looked amazed, and hiding a smile, he went on, "I know you do not intend to make a formal debut this Season, but surely the actual deed is superfluous, wouldn't you say? It appears to me, after your adventures in the country, that you are about as 'out' as any girl I have ever known."

He saw Penny was speechless; still he raised one well-gloved hand. "No, do not deny it—for I was there, if you remember."

He waited, but when Penny could only stare at him, he smiled a little. "Allow me to help you to your carriage, Miss Shaw," he said as he waved the groom away. "I shall be looking out for you at the soiree."

Penny rode home in a sort of daze, wondering why every time she saw the marquess, her body behaved in such an alarming way, making her short of breath, with her heart beating erratically, her palms damp, and her mouth dry. She did not care for it the least little bit.

True, Laurence Russell was an alarming man in many ways—that stern expression he occasionally wore—but she was not *frightened* of him. No, she was not!

And he was handsome when he smiled. It quite transformed his face. And he dressed so well! Today he had been outstanding. Everything—from his shining top hat to his dazzlingly white cravat and tasteful waistcoat, his coat of blue superfine worn over bisque breeches that fit his shapely legs like a second skin, to his highly polished boots—had been perfection.

And *he* had asked little Penny Shaw to save a dance for him! Was there anything so ridiculous?

When she reached her room to remove her bonnet before she went to see how her sister was doing, Penny was surprised to see one of the kitchen maids inside. The girl jumped as if she had been shot and quickly closed the armoire door.

"Who are you?" Penny asked, smiling. The maid looked even more frightened than Phillipa was wont to do. "And what are you doing in my room?"

The maid, a plump little thing with red hands and watery eyes, smelled of lye and grease, and Penny tried not to wrinkle her nose. She saw that she was clutching a corner of her apron between her fingers, twisting it in her agitation.

"Oh, please, miss, please! I'm only Betty. From the kitchen."

"Are you new here? I don't believe I've seen you before."

The maid dropped a curtsy. "Yes'm," she said. Then, as Penny still looked at her askance, she said in a rush, "I—I just wanted to look at your gowns. I've heard so much about them. I wasn't goin' to hurt them. They're beautiful, they are."

"Thank you. Now, don't look so frightened, Betty. I won't tell on you," Penny added kindly.

The maid curtsied again and was quick to scurry from the room. After she had gone, Penny frowned a little and went to the armoire to see if anything had been disturbed.

She noticed noting unsual, although it appeared Mrs. Bellings's cloak had been pulled forward.

Could Betty have been looking at that? she wondered as she closed the door again and went to her dressing table. Perhaps the bright color had attracted her.

Still, it did seem strange that a kitchen maid would invade the bedroom floor. Penny knew servants had their own strict protocol, and kitchen maids kept to their own domain or their attic rooms.

She turned to study her room. Yes, the upstairs maid had come and gone and tidied it. Perhaps Betty had considered this a good time to investigate gowns unlike any she would ever wear?

Even so, there was something about the incident that made Penny feel uneasy. But perhaps that was only because it might possibly involve Mrs. Bellings's cloak, and that cloak had brought such a lot of trouble to her and her family.

She almost wished there was some way she could return it to its rightful owner and have done with it once and for all.

But how could she do that? she asked herself as she smoothed her curls. She had no idea where on earth Louisa Bellings could be, and no way to find out.

Nine

THE NEXT MORNING Penny went riding in Hyde Park escorted only by a groom, for the duke had business to attend to. Although she was sorely tested, she made herself keep the mare to a sedate trot or an occasional canter, feeling very proud of herself for her forbearance.

After two circuits of the park, she told the groom she was going home. Ben Booth grinned at her and nodded. A grizzled, older man, long in the duke's service, he liked Miss Penny Shaw, for she was an excellent rider with a good seat and light hands. No need to worry she'd ruin her mare's mouth, he thought as he followed her.

To his surprise, he heard the girl give a startled cry when they reached the Stanhope Gate. Then, without a word to him, she spurred her horse into Park Lane and took off in quite the opposite direction from Berkeley Square, and at a fast trot, too.

Mumbling under his breath, Ben followed. He saw her turn into Grosvenor Place and wondered what had prompted this change of plans. But he did not become alarmed until he saw her going toward a district by the river that no genteel girl should ever frequent.

"Miss Penny!" he called, urging his horse past a heavily laden cart. "Miss Penny, stop!"

She waved her crop, but she did not obey his order. Cursing now, Ben struggled to catch her. In the crowded streets, it was all he could do to keep her little figure in its smart blue habit in sight. Once he had to pull up to avoid running a pair of urchins down, and several times he was delayed by the traffic. He muttered a number of curses as she turned into yet a narrower way. He saw she was attracting a lot of attention from the common people abroad, and his face hardened. Well, and although he'd do his best, he told himself, he wished he were twenty years younger.

He wondered who she'd seen, who she was following. No one the duke would approve of, he knew. Not if he or she lived in *this* neighborhood.

Then suddenly, Penny halted the mare. She had come out of the warren of narrow streets into a broader one, and she looked around in confusion. Relieved, Ben trotted up to her to grab her bridle.

"Miss Penny!" he said, outraged. "What'd ye go an' do that fer? Ride off like that? This is no place fer ye ter be!"

She looked at him for a moment, but he could tell she was not seeing him. "I was so sure I saw someone I am anxious to locate, riding in a hansom. But—but now it's disappeared! Oh, if only that lumbering old carriage had not held me up, I might have found her at last!"

"If she lives down this way, ye don't want ter find 'er," Ben said sternly. "Come on now, let's get out o' 'ere, afore somethin' 'appens. 'Is Grace would 'ave me 'ead if 'e knew!"

She smiled at him then. "But he won't know, Ben. How could he unless someone tells him? And nothing has happened to me."

Ben looked around and glared at some young toughs who were lounging outside a tavern, eyeing his charge. "Not yet it ain't," he said bluntly. "But that's not ter say it won't. Come along, do!"

Penny nodded obediently. They had almost

reached Park Lane again, and safety, when she was hailed by a gentleman driving a smart phaeton. Ben thanked his stars the man hadn't seen her ten minutes earlier!

As Penny rode up to the phaeton, the Marquess of Thornbury said, "Surely this is not the easiest way to get from the park to the duke's house." His voice was neither curious nor chiding, but still Penny stiffened.

"No, you are right, sir. But I thought I saw Mrs. Bellings in a hansom cab a few minutes ago, and I tried to follow her."

Thornbury's eyes grew keen. "I would hear about it, if you please. Do give your mare into your groom's keeping and take a turn in the park with me. Perry, the horses' heads," he said, and his tiger rushed to do his bidding as he got down from the perch.

Penny felt captured by his dark eyes, and without quite knowing why she obeyed him so quickly, she slid down into his waiting arms. She hoped the breathlessness she felt did not show in her voice as she bade Ben take her mare back to the stables. He looked a little doubtful, until she added, "It is all right, Ben. The marquess is a friend of the duke's, and I will be perfectly safe in his company."

As Ben nodded and turned away, leading the mare, Thornbury murmured, "And a friend of yours, too, Miss Shaw. As for being safe in my company, we must hope so, must we not?"

He lifted her into his phaeton and came around to take his own seat. As soon as he had the reins in hand, he said to his tiger, "Wait for me at the Stanhope Gate, Perry."

Penny knew enough to maintain silence until the quieter ways of the park were reached, for the marquess's team was fresh.

"Now then, you say you thought you saw Louisa Bellings?" he asked. "Where was this, and how?"

"We had just come out of the gate when she passed in an old hansom cab. I could swear it was she, even though I only saw her in profile. She was wearing the gray gown and the bonnet she had at that inn near Stanborough."

"Where did she go?"

Penny turned to stare at him, he sounded so intent. "Why, down toward the river. I managed to keep her in sight for quite some time, but I lost her at last in a maze of narrow streets."

"You had the temerity to ride down there alone? In *that* neighborhood?"

"I was not alone!" she retorted, stung by the censure she could hear so clearly in his angry voice.

He snorted. "Your groom is an old man, Miss Shaw. He'd have been no match for a pair of young toughs if they decided to rob you. Or worse," he added grimly.

"But nothing happened!" Penny protested.

"But you could not have known it would not," came the quick retort. He halted his team for a moment to stare down into her flushed face. "Are you so arrogant that you think yourself immune to the dangers in the world?" he asked, sounding as if he had gritted his teeth. He was wearing the stern look that made him look so forbidding, and Penny put up her chin.

"Of course not! I—I just didn't think . . ."

"Something women seem most reluctant to do, I believe."

When she had no reply to make to that provocative remark, he went on, "But why was it so important for you to find her?"

"I wanted to return her cloak. She obviously set great store by it, and it seemed too bad she should

118

not have it back. I would not have her think me a thief.

"But now she has disappeared again, and I've no idea where. I wish I knew where she was staying."

"You and a number of other people," he murmured as he clucked to the team. "So, you have kept the cloak, have you? Somehow, I was sure the duke would make you dispose of it."

"Well, he and my aunt Eliza tried, but I kept it on the off chance I might see Mrs. Bellings again."

He drove in silence for a few minutes. Then he said slowly, "I think it might be wise for you to put that cloak in a safe place, Miss Shaw. Don't ask me why I say so. It is just a feeling I have . . ."

"Indeed? I did not think men believed in *intuition*, being so logical and *thoughtful* by nature."

"Sometimes it is wise to listen to feelings, whatever your sex," he told her as they reached the gate and he paused to let his tiger jump up behind. As he turned into Curzon Street, he said, "I wish I had the power to forbid you to try and contact Louisa Bellings again. Such action might well be dangerous. But I suppose you will go your own way, and sooner or later, probably sooner, find yourself in serious trouble."

Penny looked indignant. "I cannot imagine why both you and my uncle seem to expect me to fall into that condition all the time."

Thornbury halted the phaeton before the duke's house then. Not waiting for him to come around to assist her, Penny scrambled down by herself. Looking back up at him where he sat frowning at her, she said, "Thank you for the drive, m'lord. And please do not concern yourself with me. I am quite competent to see to my own welfare."

As he touched his hat to her, he said, "Yes, and pigs might fly! Give you good day, ma'am."

Before Penny could think of a suitably scathing

reply, he drove off, leaving her clenching her fists and glaring after him. As she marched up the steps and sounded the knocker, she thought Thornbury quite the most impossible man she had ever met. And as Tuttle admitted her and she remembered to smile at him, she wondered who the marquess thought he was, anyway. Her welfare was none of his concern. Why, he was not even a relative!

Phillipa called her then from the head of the stairs, and she put the troublesome marquess from her mind.

Still, when she was getting ready for bed late that evening, she remembered what he had said to her, and as soon as she had dismissed her maid, she took the scarlet cloak from the depths of the armoire. She inspected it carefully inside and out, but she could find nothing unusual about it. Still, Thornbury had said she should keep it safe. And then there had been that kitchen maid's possible interest in it. Penny folded the cloak carefully and looked around. It didn't appear there was any hiding place in her room that would not be easy to detect, and she hardly liked to wander the halls in her night robe and dressing gown. A maid or a footman might see her. I'll put it somewhere else tomorrow, she promised herself as she slipped it under her mattress.

Several hours later, Penny woke with the most peculiar feeling she was not alone. Afraid to even look, she strained to listen. Not a sound could be heard, yet still the feeling that someone was there persisted. She forced herself to open her eyes, and she stifled a gasp when she saw a figure holding a lit candle stub backing away from the armoire. A male figure, she noted, dressed all in black with a mask hiding his features.

Her first instinct was to scream at the top of her

lungs, but something cautioned her that if she did so, it might be even more dangerous than her present situation. The man—whoever he was—did not appear interested in her, thank heavens!

Lying rigid, her eyes followed the intruder as he inspected the chest at the foot of the bed, then went into the dressing room. It was truly amazing how quiet he was, she thought. He made not a single, infinitesimal sound.

Even as she wondered if she would have time to jump out of bed, race to the door, and escape, he returned. As he approached her at last, Penny closed her eyes and tried to quiet her thumping heart. And she prayed harder than she had ever prayed.

A moment later, she heard the door to the hall open and shut, and she threw back the covers and ran to lock it. Only then did she begin to scream. And only when she heard doors opening along the hall, the servants clattering down the attic stairs, did she stop.

Her hands were trembling so now, she had trouble unlocking her door, but when at last she succeeded, her uncle was standing in the hall. He was wearing a brilliant paisley dressing gown over his nightshirt, holding a branch of candles high in one hand while he brandished a poker with the other. Penny also saw her aunt scurrying into Phillipa's room, and, reminded of her sister for the first time, she groaned. But what else could she have done? she argued to herself as her heart still pounded in her breast.

"What's to do, Penny?" the duke demanded. With his stern glare and ruffled white hair, he was a fearsome sight.

"There was . . . someone . . . in my room . . . searching it!" Penny gasped. She saw her uncle looked sceptical, and she took a deep breath and added quickly, "There was! I saw him plain! He was dressed all in black and masked! But never mind that. Perhaps we can catch him before he escapes the house. We must hurry!"

By this time, a sizable number of the servants had arrived on the scene. Two of the maids were clutching each other and sobbing, and one of the footmen was trying to hide behind his fellows, so he could do up the buttons of his breeches.

"Your Grace?" Tuttle asked, as he elbowed his way forward.

In any other situation, Penny would have been hard put not to laugh. Mr. Tuttle sounded unruffled, and he was properly attired in breeches and shirt. He had even put his jacket on, but he had not lingered long enough to don his hose and shoes. His thin, white hairy legs and calloused red feet added nothing to his dignity. Penny saw he had a bunion, and she was sorry for him.

"Set the footmen to searching the house from this floor to the cellars," the duke ordered. "Tell them to arm themselves with something. We've had a housebreaker."

As the butler went to give his orders, the duke turned again to his niece and said, "Not that I think we'll catch him, mind. He's had plenty of time to make good his escape by now. Still, we can but try. Tuttle!"

As the butler came back, he said, "You will come with me while I inspect the rooms for anything missing. The rest of you might just as well go back to bed. Good night."

His cold, even words were like a dousing in cold water. The maids stopped sobbing abruptly, the excited whispering died away, and everyone meekly filed from the hall.

"First, let us look in my niece's room," Longford said. Penny led the way, going to the dressing table to light the branch of candles there.

"Did you notice him taking anything?" Longford asked her.

She shook her head, and he added, "What exactly did he do?"

"When I woke up, I saw him over by the armoire," Penny said, sitting down abruptly and trying to control her violent trembling. That was strange, she thought. She had not trembled as badly as this before! "Then he went through the chest there, and looked the dressing room over. But he didn't have anything with him when he left. I—I screamed as soon as I had my door locked."

"But whatever could he have been after in *here*?" the duke asked no one in particular. "I would have thought he'd go for the plate—other valuables—money that might be kept in the library. But to search a young girl's room! It's not as if you had a fortune in jewels hidden away."

He paused then as if another thought had occurred to him. "But perhaps he thought this was my room?" he said.

"No, he knew it was mine," Penny said. "He—he came up to the bed and stared down at me. *Brr!*"

Her uncle seemed to notice how she hugged herself then, how her teeth were chattering, and he frowned. "Get back into bed before you catch your death, niece! Tuttle, have one of the maids bring Miss Penny a hot drink for the shock. And then you go to sleep, my dear. There'll be no repeat of this, my word on it."

Penny told herself she would have liked to trail her uncle as he searched the house, but meekly, she did as she was told. She was so cold!

After investigating, the duke could find nothing missing. And Tuttle told him when he came to the library later that the robber had made good his escape.

"The footmen found where he got in—and out,

Your Grace," he said, sounding agitated. "A cellar window had been left unlatched. I'm sure I don't know how that happened. You know I inspect them regularly."

Longford frowned, turning a quill this way and that in his hands as he sat behind his desk. "Could it be that someone in the house unlatched that window deliberately?" he asked softly. "Who is new in my service?"

Tuttle coughed a little. "There's only the housekeeper's nephew who serves as boot boy, Your Grace. I'm sure Mrs. Gillian can vouch for him. Oh, yes, and I believe there was a new scullery maid come a month or so back. Would you care to question them?"

"Not now. It's almost four. I'll see everyone in the morning."

As the butler bowed, the duke rose and added, "And Tuttle, don't be too hard on yourself. It was not your fault. Just find out what you can about this scullery maid . . . there's a good fellow."

But in the morning, Betty was nowhere to be found. She had dressed with the other maids and gone to the kitchen, but later she had not returned from a trip to the privy. Her room was searched, but outside of a few old gowns and shifts, nothing identifying where she had come from, or where she might have gone, could be discovered.

Knowing how futile it would be to search for her, Longford summoned a private investigator, to hire him and some of his men to guard the house at night. Whoever had been in here had been looking for something, he knew. He might try to return. And feeling as weary as he did this morning, and every one of his sixty-one years, he did not care for a repeat performance.

Phillipa remained in bed, still in shock from waking in the dark to hear her sister's bloodcurdling screams, and still afraid that robbers and rapists might be loose here.

"I told her she was being a ninny, but you know Phil," Penny told her uncle as she sat with him and her aunt for nuncheon.

Lady Eliza bristled in defense of her pet. "I am sure it was only to be expected after that horrible din you set up in the middle of the night!" she said tartly. "It was just like you to behave so! Yet knowing how high-strung your sister is, I wonder that even you could . . ."

"Would you have advised her to stifle her screams, Lizzy? Could you have done so if *you* had discovered a masked man in your room?" the duke asked. "Would you have stood by and let all of us be murdered in our beds, perhaps? Try for a little sense, woman! Phillipa will take no harm from this, and you may tell her she may be easy. The house will be guarded by professionals from now on. There is nothing to worry about."

"I'm afraid that won't do a bit of good," Penny said as she put her knife and fork down. "Every time she hears a floor creak, or a window rattle, she'll be sure they are back. It is too bad! She won't even go to the Kincaid soiree this evening."

"Of course she will not in her shattered condition," Lady Eliza said, glaring at her difficult, willful niece. "Nor shall you, for I must remain with darling Phillipa, and so cannot chaperon you."

Penny opened her mouth to protest, and then wondered why she felt so strongly about attending yet another boring, endless evening in a stuffy mansion, surrounded by all the fops and fools of the ton.

"There is no reason for Penny to beg off, too," the duke said as he signaled a properly attired Tuttle to clear the table. "I shall escort her myself."

Lady Eliza looked indignant that her least favorite niece was to have the treat, but Penny smiled at her uncle and nodded her delight.

She wore her new blue gown to the party, and had her maid do up her curls with a matching ribbon. She was sorry she only had a locket to wear, but even so, she was pleased with her appearance when she ran down the stairs to join her uncle.

"I've not seen this before," Longford said as he draped her navy satin cloak over her shoulders. "It is handsome."

"Deirdre chose it for me," Penny said, wrinkling her nose at him. "You know I have no interest in finery."

As the two left the house for their waiting carriage, Penny saw a large man lounging against the palings nearby, and she whispered, "Is that one of your guards, sir? He certainly looks formidable enough!"

"Yes, and there are two more in back. They remain on duty till dawn, and for as many more nights as we need them. I trust their presence will eventually reassure Phillipa."

There was such a crush of traffic that they had to wait quite a while before their carriage could inch forward to the red carpet that covered the front steps of Mrs. Kincaid's mansion. It appeared she had invited all London society to her soiree. Penny knew Deirdre and her husband were to attend, and she was reassured by that, for she knew few people. And, she told herself, even though she scorned such evenings, it was not at all comfortable to spend the entire time alone—trying to look as if you were enjoying yourself.

After she and the duke had greeted their hostess, a charming older lady who had a special smile for Longford, to Penny's vast amusement, they followed the crowd to the ballroom. The duke introduced her to several young people, and when the dancing started, she was happy to have a partner. True, Sir Hevron was only a few years older than she was herself, and he tended to stammer when he spoke, but he was a partner.

Sometime later, she was surprised to see Alastair Pettibone coming toward her, a wide smile on his face.

"Miss Shaw," he said as he bowed over her hand. "Dare I hope you have a dance left?"

Penny opened her mouth to refuse him as coldly as she could, but he whispered harshly, "I must speak to you. Do not deny me!"

Intrigued, she agreed, but instead of leading her forward to join the set that was just forming, he took her to a sofa set a little apart from any others, then seated her.

"Well, what do you want?" Penny demanded.

He looked around nervously. "Are you always so abrupt?" he asked in an undertone. "I just wanted to say how happy I am you reached your uncle's home unscathed, and to beg your pardon again for the mistake my grooms made."

Although this was a handsome apology, Penny only nodded slightly.

"I daresay none of this would have happened if you had not pinched Louisa's scarlet cloak," he went on, shaking his head.

"I did *not* pinch it! I borrowed it by mistake!"

"Oh, yes, of course. No need to fly up in the boughs about it, is there? You are the most prickly girl! By the way, do you still have that cloak?"

Penny stared at him suspiciously. "Why do you ask? It is not yours."

"No, but I could return it to the lady. I am sure you do not want to keep someone else's property, now do you?"

"I do not have the cloak anymore," Penny lied, crossing her fingers under cover of a fold in her gown. And then she wondered why she had told such a whisker. Was it only because she did not like Alastair Pettibone, or was it more than that—that she did not trust him? She wondered where his cousin, the marquess, was, and looked around for him. He was nowhere in sight.

"You don't have it? What happened to it?" Pettibone demanded.

"I gave it to one of the maids. My aunt took such a dislike to it, you see, she said she'd not have it in the house. And I didn't have the least expectation of ever seeing Mrs. Bellings again."

He sat silent for a moment, staring out at the dancers with unseeing eyes.

"Which maid?" he asked, all pretense of cordiality gone from his voice.

Penny stiffened. "Surely you overstep yourself, sir! If Mrs. Bellings applies to me, I shall of course reimburse her for her garment. I fail to see why you concern yourself in an affair that is none of your business! And now you must excuse me. Lady Manning is waiting for me."

He grasped her arm for a moment, but one look at her indignant face and sparkling eyes, and he dropped it at once. "Please," he said softly. "Tell me the name of the maid you gave it to."

Penny rose quickly. "I shall do nothing of the sort! And I do not care to talk to you any longer."

As she walked away from him, Alastair Pettibone stared after her, a frown on his long, thin face. Some little distance away, where he was standing with a group of gentlemen, the Marquess of Thornbury watched him carefully. He wondered what his cousin had been saying to Penny Shaw to anger her so, for even from this distance there had been no mistaking that emotion on her face. Then he shrugged. He would find out as soon as he spoke to her.

Penny went to sit beside her cousin. In only a few minutes she was regaling her with an account of the doings late last night at the duke's house, and Deirdre sat enthralled through the telling.

"But what on earth was the robber after, do you suppose?" she asked. Then she waved her fan. "That was a silly thing to ask! Of course you can have no idea. But Penny, how frightened you must have been, even though I am sure you hid it well. You know, I perceive my father-in-law was right. You do seem to attract trouble, do you not?"

"I don't mean to, Deirdre, honestly I don't," Penny protested. "Things just seem to happen to me, and I wish they wouldn't! Besides, it upsets Phil so, and now Lady Eliza is furious with me again. Oh, why, *why* can't I be like other girls? I'm sure not a single one in this room has ever had to deal with a housebreaker!"

Deirdre chuckled. "No, but I daresay they lead such uneventful lives, the poor dears must be terribly bored! Perhaps you should consider yourself fortunate?"

"Are you bamming me, Deirdre?" Penny demanded.

Before she could reply, a warm baritone interrupted. "Lady Manning, your servant. I hope you have saved me that dance you promised me, Miss Shaw?"

Penny looked up to see the Marquess of Thornbury bowing to her and holding out his hand, and without a word to her companion, she rose and gave him hers.

As the two went away, Deirdre Shaw's expression was very thoughtful. My, my, Thornbury! she reflected. Whoever would have imagined it? I wonder if the duke knows?

Ten

LIKE HIS COUSIN, Laurence Russell had no intention of wasting his time with Miss Shaw, dancing. But unlike Pettibone, he took her out of the ballroom to an antechamber nearby. There was no one in the room, and he nodded in satisfaction as he seated her and went to pour them both a glass of wine from a decanter set on a table against the wall. Penny saw he had not closed the door; she assumed there could be no impropriety in being alone with him in that case, and she was grateful to him for his thoughtfulness.

"I saw you talking to my cousin a short while ago," Thornbury began abruptly. "What did he want?"

"I do not know what it is about your family, sir, that makes every male member of it question me so unceasingly!" she said, all kindly feelings for him gone in a thrice.

He smiled at her then, and raised his glass in a silent toast. Penny told herself that this time, no matter what he said—or did—she would not lose her temper. No, nor succumb to damp palms and a fast-beating heart, either. But she admitted it would have been easier to keep to her resolution if he had sat across from her, instead of close beside her.

"I was watching you both, and I saw how he angered you. Surely, as head of the family, I have a right to know why? I might be required to ask him to beg your pardon. One never knows."

Penny sighed and accepted defeat. For several minutes she spoke quietly about her conversation with Alastair Pettibone. As she did so, Thornbury caressed his jaw with a large, well-cared-for hand.

"I must admit I was surprised to see him here this evening," he mused when she fell silent at last. "He does not generally attend such affairs."

"I have a theory about that, for we had a housebreaker last night, and he searched my room."

Thornbury turned, his fine dark eyes intent on her face. "You were there at the time?"

"Of course! It was very late, and I was asleep. But a premonition woke me up and I discovered him there. He was looking for something.

"Tell me, is it not entirely possible that your cousin was the housebreaker, and not having any luck last night, decided to apply to me directly?"

Penny sat back, proud of herself for having come up with such an ingenious solution, and in such a well-considered, *thoughtful* way, too. But to her dismay, Thornbury only began to laugh, long and helplessly.

"Whyever do you laugh? It is not funny!" she said, longing to shake him. "And I'm sure it is logical, considering Mr. Pettibone's interest in the cloak tonight!"

"If it were another man, perhaps, but not my cousin. He would be too afraid he might be caught and ruined. Besides, I doubt he would even know how to gain admittance to a locked mansion. And if he should by any luck bumble inside, he would have been sure to upset a small table, walk into a door, or fall down a flight of stairs in the dark. You did not mention any noise. That speaks of a professional.

"But come, permit me to tell you—you are all

abroad in your suppositions. Perhaps Alastair only wanted the cloak back as a way to get back into Mrs. Bellings's good graces.

"You have it safe?"

"Yes, last night I had it hidden under my mattress, but this morning I found a better place for it. And no, I've no intention of telling you where it is, so there!"

His brows rose. "I have not the slightest interest in its location," he said at his haughtiest. "One would think you considered *me* a suspect."

Penny found herself blushing, and hated herself for it. "Of course I do not; do not be absurd!" she said hastily.

He chuckled then, good humor restored, and raised his glass to lay it against her flushed cheek. It was cool on her skin, and Penny looked at him, startled.

"Do you know, you look just like a startled fawn. A fawn with deep blue eyes, that is," he said as he removed the glass.

"I suppose your sister had hysterics last night, and that is why she does not accompany you here?"

"Yes, she was quite overcome. And even though uncle has men guarding the house now, she cannot be reassured. I am afraid she is not very brave."

Thornbury clamped his lips together, lest he tell Miss Shaw that that was an understatement if ever he had heard one.

"Why did you tell Alastair that you had disposed of the cloak?" he asked instead.

She looked perplexed. "I have no idea. The words were out of my mouth before I had time to consider them seriously. And you must forgive me, but there is something about your cousin . . . I mean, I . . ."

She fell silent in confusion, and he patted her hand. "I know. It is unnecessary to tell me. But come, the music has stopped. No doubt you are awaited in the ballroom for the next dance?"

"No, I'm not," Penny said, as honest as she had always been. "I did have a few partners earlier, but there is no one for the rest of the evening."

She blushed again and rose so hastily she almost tripped on the hem of her gown. "I intend to go to Deirdre . . . er . . . I mean, Lady Manning."

Slowly he rose to put her glass and his on a tray. "You must allow me to escort you to her, ma'am. And perhaps we might share a dance later on?"

Penny was sure her face was as scarlet as Mrs. Bellings's cloak. Of course he had to ask her now, after she had as much as pleaded with him to do so—by revealing her unfilled dance card.

"I don't think so," she said, hating herself—and him, in equal proportion. "I am feeling weary after all the excitement and loss of sleep last night. But I do thank you, sir."

He did not seem at all distressed to be refused, and Penny's feelings changed from chagrin to indignation that he could so easily chat of innocuous things as they went back to the festivities. But still, she knew she had not handled their encounter with any degree of sophistication, and that annoyed her as well. It was obvious the marquess considered her a naughty, unruly child, for he almost always spoke to her as if she were. And she had just confirmed this opinion by her gauche behavior. Oh, when would she ever learn?

They had barely stepped inside the ballroom again before a tall, loose-limbed gentleman came forward to bow to them.

"Thornbury, your servant," he said, smiling a little at Penny.

She did not smile in return. Lordy, lordy! Here was the man who had seen her in the carriage at Alastair Pettibone's country home! But perhaps he did not recognize her? Pray he had not!

"Whitaker," the marquess was saying. "Allow me

133

to present Miss Penelope Shaw, Duke Longford's niece. Bartholomew Whitaker, ma'am."

Penny curtsied, her eyes downcast, so she missed the surprise on the gentleman's pleasant face. When she dared to look at him again, he had his features under firm control.

"My pleasure, Miss Shaw. You are newly arrived in town? I do not believe I have seen you before."

"Yes," Penny said baldly, praying he spoke the truth. "I am come with my sister for the Season."

"London is honored," Whitaker said, with a little grin.

It was then Penny knew that he had recognized her. She said not another word, and after a few minutes of casual chat, the marquess excused them, to take her to her cousin.

"You are suddenly very quiet," he observed, staring down at her. "But perhaps you really are tired, as you claimed? Now I thought that a clanker, knowing your fortitude as well as I do, but life is full of surprises, is it not?

"Ah, Lady Manning! Here is your cousin, safely returned to you. Have a care for the child. She is not feeling herself this evening."

Penny glared at his broad-shouldered back as he went away, but not a one of Deirdre's eager questions could get her to confess a single thing that had happened. Not with Thornbury, and most assuredly not the disastrous meeting with this Mr. Whitaker, who had seen her only a short time ago, unchaperoned, in the company of two men who were not even relatives. Penny saw her family's reputation and Phillipa's future going to hell in a hand basket, and she wanted to die.

The evening was the longest she had ever known.

It was very late when the duke and Penny returned to Berkeley Square. Longford paused to speak to the man on duty at the front before he helped his niece up the steps.

"Has there been any trouble?" she asked as they waited for Tuttle to admit them.

"No, none at all. I suspect our intruder has given up that avenue, or if he has not, was frightened away by the guards when he saw them.

"But tell me, Penny—did you have a good time this evening?"

"Part of it," Penny said honestly. "I am not used to such things, and some people are not kind, or at all friendly. But I do admit I enjoy listening to their absurdities. Such fussing over fashions, such interest in scandal!"

"There are foolish people everywhere. Deirdre tells me you danced with Thornbury—Ah, Tuttle. You may lock the house now, dismiss the footmen.

"Well, child?"

"We did not dance. We only talked a little while. But sir, even though I know he is a friend of yours, I cannot like him. He treats me as if—as if I were no more than two and ten!"

"Ah, I see," her uncle said, a twinkle deep in his eyes as he flicked her cheek with one finger. "Run along to bed, my dear. You must be tired. And do not concern yourself with Thornbury. He is not so very old himself, you know."

Some distance away in Pall Mall, the gentleman they were discussing sat before a dying fire, nursing a snifter of brandy as he considered the events of the evening.

What was Alastair's sudden interest in the cloak? he wondered. Had he found Louisa Bellings? He himself had set his agent to searching the district where Penny had last seen her, but the man had had no luck locating her so far.

And what was there about that cloak that had so many people intent on its recovery? Perhaps there was something hidden in it? Something Louisa Bellings needed before she could blackmail Alastair?

Or perhaps something she could use to blackmail someone else? He reviewed all of Alastair's cronies that he knew and shook his head, frowning now. Most of them were silly fellows intent only on pleasure, but there were one or two others. Young Dickson at the Foreign Office, for example. He had often wondered how the man had ever become a secretary there, he was so indiscreet. Had Dickson given Alastair something incriminating? Something someone would pay dearly for to get back? He knew Alastair would have leapt at the chance to get a march on the rest of the world, be first with the news. It made him feel important.

But there had been no hint of a new scandal, Thornbury knew, for he had been listening for it. Not a word about important papers gone astray, war plans revealed.

The intruder at the duke's home bothered him excessively. To think that spirited little girl had been in danger! To think there had been a desperate man in her room while she lay helpless in bed! It made his blood run cold. And she had looked so pretty tonight—quite grownup, in fact—in a blue gown the color of her eyes, with her unruly curls tamed. He never saw them without recalling how they had been at first meeting, a rich profusion tumbling over her shoulders. She had behaved well, too, tonight. Anyone who did not know her would have thought her just another demure debutante, for she had done nothing to call attention to herself. He chuckled. How hard that must have been for her!

Then he remembered how silent she had become, how wooden, when he had introduced her to Bartholomew Whitaker. Had she peeked out that carriage in the country, after all, and seen him? And he, her?

Yawning, the marquess finished his brandy, rose, and stretched. He'd get no further with this puzzle tonight. Perhaps the light of day, and a good night's sleep, would help.

Someone else was thinking about that cloak, too. A few streets away, Alastair Pettibone paced up and down his rooms, gnawing a thumbnail. So, she had given the cloak away, had she? And she wouldn't tell him where it might be found? Pray God she had done so, for with the cloak missing, Louisa had no way of making mischief!

It had taken a long time for Alastair to reach the same conclusion his cousin had, but at last he had come to see, when Louisa made no move, that she had to have hidden the evidence in her cloak. And that was why she had been so upset she had screamed obscenities at the Shaw ladies when she had lost it. But if the cloak never came to light, he was free and clear. There was nothing she could do.

For a moment, he toyed with the idea of questioning the duke's female servants, but he quickly discarded it. That would be too risky; it was best to let sleeping dogs lie. Best to hope that luck would be with him for once, and no one would ever know of his involvement. And it was the easiest way out, too.

The next morning brought Penny a note from Lady Manning asking her to bring Phillipa to her home that same afternoon at four—and begging her not to fail. "For if you remember, my dear," she wrote,

I have a plan, and all the pieces are now in place. And if Phillipa is still cringing under her covers, tell her we are to have a nursery tea, just the three of us and the children. That will fetch her!

Penny looked up from her note to where her sister sat toying with a piece of toast. They were alone in the sunny breakfast room, Lady Eliza having gone to tell the housekeeper that it was surely unnecessary—to say nothing of extravagant!—to serve dinners with three courses and so many removes.

Penny thought Phillipa looked as well as she always had, but she had noticed that whenever a door closed somewhere, or a strange voice was heard in the hall, she started and paled.

"Here is a note from Deirdre, inviting us to tea today," she said brightly. "And it is such a lovely day, too, Phil—so sunny and warm. It would do you good to get out of the house for some fresh air."

"Oh, I really don't feel up to it," Phillipa whispered, raising her handkerchief to her lips. "Please don't make me go!"

"Goose! As if I could!" Penny said, wrinkling her nose at her. "But it is a shame you must miss the treat. Deirdre writes she is having the children join us, and no one else. And you know how you dote on them. Besides, I am sure they are missing you, you have been such a constant caller. But of course," she went on as she buttered another muffin, "if you do not feel you can go, that is the end of it."

"There won't be anybody else there?" Phillipa asked.

"No. Just family."

"Well, in that case, I suppose I could manage," Phillipa said, just as Penny and Deirdre had known she would. "Those dear little boys!"

"What is it about children that appeals to you so, Phil?" Penny asked seriously. "I mean, I like them, too, but not as much as you do."

"I don't know exactly," her sister admitted. "I just know I feel easy in their company, and happy. And the things they say and do make me laugh. I—I wish I had babies."

"Well, you'll have to get a husband first," her practical sister reminded her. "I hope you do—and have lots of babies. You would make a wonderful mother. Of course, I'm not sure I'll be much of an aunt, but I'm willing to try!"

She saw Phillipa was blushing rosy at the idea, and she smiled to herself. Phil was so silly! She knew it took two to make babies, even if neither of them were quite clear about how that happened.

Later that afternoon, they were driven to Deirdre's house in the duke's carriage. Penny was glad her sister had chosen to wear her pretty sprigged muslin, although she was sure it would be sadly crushed by the time the tea party was over. Deirdre's little boys were just as rambunctious as any others. Still, she hoped their company would cheer Phil up. Even with the coachman and two grooms for protection, she still cringed back in her seat and was exceedingly pale.

It only took a few minutes in the children's company for her to lose that frightened look, and only a few minutes more before she had removed her bonnet and gloves and taken baby James on her lap.

When the boys had been brought down by their nursemaids, three-year-old George had exclaimed, "Pippa! Pippa! I not see you in so long! Where you been?"

Matthew Shaw, very proper at five, had looked disgusted. "Don't you know any better, you baby? You're s'pposed to bow and greet Cousin Penny, too."

"I do hope Matthew isn't going to turn into a prig," Deirdre murmured to Penny as her sons crowded around Phillipa, both talking at once. "But look at her, Penny. Did you ever see such a picture?"

"She told me this morning that she wished she had babies, lots of them," Penny confided. Deirdre chuckled.

For a miracle, teatime was accomplished without a serious accident, although Matthew and George argued about who should have the last Queen cake. Penny solved that problem by eating it herself.

"Oh, do say the children may stay longer, ma'am," Phillipa begged as the tea cart was wheeled away. "I want to tell them a fairy tale."

"Of course, dear," her cousin agreed, with a sunny smile. "Why don't you take them over by the window and sit on the floor with them? It will be so cozy, and I've something I wish to discuss with Penny."

"I wish I knew what you were up to," Penny complained when the others were out of earshot. "You have the most devilish, pleased-with-yourself look!"

"You shall find out any minute. Ah, yes. I thought I heard the knocker. Now just watch, Penny!"

The door to the salon opened, and the Manning's butler ushered a tall young gentleman inside. "Mr. Christopher Blakely, ma'am," he said.

"Cousin Chris!" Deirdre exclaimed, jumping to her feet. "Why, what a surprise!"

The gentleman looked astounded, as well he might, for he had been invited for four forty-five, not a minute sooner or later, but before he could say anything, she rushed on, "Let me make you known to my newly met cousins. This is Miss Penelope Shaw, and over there, with the children, is Miss Phillipa Shaw."

The gentleman bowed to Penny, and she smiled in response, liking the look of him immediately. He

140

was not a handsome man, but he had a pleasant face, wavy chestnut hair, and hazel eyes with a distinct twinkle in them. Even so, there was sadness there, too, and perhaps a maturity that sat well on his young shoulders.

She glanced over at Phil, to see she had gone quite pale again. Goose! she thought impatiently. She knew her sister was distressed that a stranger had caught her seated on the floor, her gown mussed and her blond curls ruffled from the baby's hands. Too bad she does not see what a delightful picture she makes, Penny thought.

Mr. Blakely seemed to think so, too, for he studied her for quite a long time.

"Pippa! Pippa! Go on with the story!" George demanded.

"Pippa?" Mr. Blakely asked, smiling at her. "But what a charming nickname, Miss Shaw. It suits you."

"George had trouble pronouncing Phillipa," his hostess told him as she indicated a chair that faced the group by the window. "Do sit down, Chris. Phillipa is telling them a story, but it will soon be over."

"I hope you're not planning on banishing them then," he said as he took the seat. "I have not seen them for such a long time."

"That is so. Very well, they may stay, although no doubt Nanny will say I spoil them. She always does, whenever I indulge them. I wish she did not terrorize me so!"

Penny giggled, and he turned to her. "It is just that I cannot imagine anyone terrorizing Deirdre, can you, sir?" she explained.

Deirdre told Mr. Blakely all the news of town, said she hoped he would stay for a long visit, and kept the conversation light until, at last, a reluctant Phillipa brought the children to join them. The little boys abandoned her for their masculine cousin then, and still holding the baby, she gave the viscountess and her sister a reproachful look.

"Enough, enough, you monkeys!" He laughed as George tried to climb his arm and Matthew bombarded him with questions. "Remember your manners!"

"How are your twins, Chris?" Deirdre asked.

"They are fine," he said, his face sobering. "Not quite the size of young James there, but doing nicely."

"I should tell you girls that Chris has the most adorable pair of twins, the same age as my James. Little Andrew and Amy are so delightful."

"Oh, do you have twins, sir?" Phillipa asked, her face lighting up. "A year and a half is a wonderful age for babies, is it not? And do they have your hair and eyes?"

He nodded, looking bemused. Penny was a little perplexed as to Deirdre's motives, for what was the sense of introducing Phil to a married man? It was not long, however, before she learned of his wife's death in childbirth, and although she was sorry for him, she now saw her cousin's plan plain.

"I am so sorry," Phillipa said softly, her blue eyes filling with tears. "How sad for you and your babies."

He nodded, looking stunned at her sympathy as the nursemaids came in for the children. George would have protested, but Mr. Blakely said he would come by tomorrow and take them for a drive in the park, and peace was restored.

"Pippa must come, too," George announced as he jerked a bow. "I 'sist!"

"Now, George, I can't do that," Phillipa protested, rosy with embarrassment.

"Certainly you can," Deirdre scolded her. "For I shall come, too. What a shame you have a fitting tomorrow, Penny, and so must miss the treat," she added, turning slightly to wink at her. With a great effort, Penny suppressed a gurgle of amusement.

A time was set, and the two Shaw girls rose to say good-bye. Penny saw how Mr. Blakely's eyes lingered on her sister's face, his special smile for her. Could you fall in love like that? she wondered as she led the way to the carriage. In an instant? How strange!

Phillipa was very quiet once the carriage began to take them home.

"I do hope you are not going to accuse me of tricking you, Phil," Penny tried to say lightly. "But I had no idea Mr. Blakely would be there. Truly."

"Hmmm?" Phillipa said absentmindedly. "Oh, no. I am sure you did not. But isn't it sad, Penny? He's so young to have lost his wife. And to be left with those two little babies! Poor man!"

"Yes, it is sad," Penny said, carefully choosing her words. "He seems so nice, too, don't you think? So pleasant and congenial."

Phillipa only nodded a little before she turned to look out the carriage window.

Wisely Penny did not try to pursue the matter further.

Eleven

A COUNCIL OF war was held at April's little house that same afternoon. Her protector had been called out of town for a few days, and curious, she had relented and let Blackie meet Louisa there.

"No luck?" Louisa asked as he swaggered into the parlor and looked around for a seat. He was so huge, the room seemed a great deal smaller than it was.

"No luck, curse it!" he growled as he took the sturdiest chair and frowned at them both.

April frowned right back at him from her seat near the fire, but it was Louisa Bellings who continued to question him, standing before him, hands on hips.

"I told you it would be too dangerous to break into a duke's house!" she scolded. "But you wouldn't listen! What if your man had been taken? What would have happened to us then?"

"Benny'd not rat. 'E knows wot would 'appen ter 'im if 'e did."

"But why did you use him, anyway?" Louisa persisted.

" 'Ad ter. That maid was so feared after miss caught 'er in 'er room, she wouldn't 'elp no more. But she did say the cloak was there. Saw it, she did. But when Benny searched fer it, it 'ad disappeared. Think that young missy's on ter the game?"

144

"How should I know?" Louisa muttered, sitting down at last.

"What I'd like to know is, why you didn't just *ask* her for it outright, in the beginning," April contributed. The others stared at her in amazement.

"All right, so you screamed at her aunt and sister, but you didn't scream at *her*," she explained. "And you could have written her a nice, ladylike note asking her to return it. Bet she'd have done it in a minute. She's the niece of a duke, not a common thief."

Louisa's laugh was harsh and grating.

"I believe you are right, April," she said at last. "I outsmarted myself, didn't I? Because I certainly could have done just what you said, and the girl probably remembered me fondly. After all, I invited her to share my bed, so she wouldn't have to sleep on a pallet on the floor."

"I still don't understand what prompted you to be so charitable," April told her. "It's not a bit like you to put yourself out. For a stranger, I mean," she added hastily as Louisa shot her a venomous glance.

"It was no trouble to me, and I rather thought I might get in the family's good graces. Perhaps use them when I got to town. Of course, I didn't know they were so exalted. No one of that quality ever stops at a place like the Fox and Grapes.

"Too bad I didn't think of such a simple solution earlier. And now Blackie's broken into the house, alerted her, there'll be no making her give it up. Damn you, man! Why did you do it? I told you and told you, *no!*"

" 'Ere now, none o' that!" he growled, clenching his fists.

Louisa subsided.

"I did wot I thought would 'elp. More than yer doin', seems ter me."

There was a little silence, pregnant with under-currents, and when Louisa spoke, her voice was cold. "I remind you, Blackie—this is my lay, not yours. You will get your money for helping me, but I make the plans here. And I won't have you doing things without consulting with me first. Do you understand?"

She sounded as menacing as Blackie ever had, and he smiled a little, showing yellowed teeth. "No need ter get up on yer 'igh 'orse, woman. I agree it's yer lay. But wot are we ter do now? I sent Benny back there last night, an' 'e found the 'ouse guarded front an' back. There'll be no gettin' in there no more.

"Mayhap it'll come down ter kidnappin' after all."

"I don't know. I'll have to think about it," Louisa muttered.

Blackie rose. "Well, let me know when yer done thinkin'. I've better things ter do than wait on yer, ye know."

Louisa did not watch him as he swaggered out. They could hear his rumbling voice in the hall as he spoke to Nan. A moment later, the front door slammed behind him.

"*Brrr*," April said, rubbing her arms. "He gives me the shivers. Always has, always will. Hope you know what you're about, Louisa, using him. You may say this is your lay, but Blackie is apt to go his own way. And if he decides to get the cloak himself, and cut you out, he'll do it in a minute. And you know he'd as soon murder you as look at you."

For the first time, Louisa Bellings looked amused. "No, he won't do that. I told him right at the beginning that I'd left a letter with someone he doesn't know, explaining everything. If anything happens to me, that letter goes to the authorities. And Blackie's name is in it.

"I made a mistake letting him in on this," she admitted. "But it's too late to cut him out now. For one thing, he knows too much, and for another, he'd not stand for it.

"Do you have a pistol, April?"

"No, no. I don't. What would I want with one?" the little blonde asked, looking frightened. "And why do you want one?"

Louisa smiled. "Shall we say for protection? That sounds so much better than having it to make Blackie behave himself. I will have to buy one, I guess—and there's no time like the present."

"Why don't we treat ourselves to a nice evening out?" April asked. "M'lord won't have to know anything about it, and there's a demimonde's ball tonight."

Louisa shook her head. "Not for me, there isn't, with Alastair Pettibone searching all over town for me. And if I were you, I'd stay away, too. Some friends of your protector's might be there, and if they see you, they'll be only too happy to tell him about it, mark my words."

April pouted, but she could see the wisdom of what Louisa said, and she resigned herself to another boring night at home.

Penny thought her sister strangely reticent after her drive in the park with Christopher Blakely, Deirdre, and the children, and she wondered at it, although she did not pry.

She herself had remained at home in the duke's library, reading a good book, although in reality she was hiding from her aunt. Lady Eliza had been full of questions about this outing of her pet's—and without her sister, too—and Penny did not intend to tell her a single thing, lest she ruin what appeared to be a most promising beginning by warning Phillipa off widowed gentlemen who used

innocent children to lure young girls to a life of un-
remitting servitude.

From some of the things her aunt Eliza had said
ever since they had arrived in town, Penny sensed
she did not want Phillipa to marry, at least not for
some years yet. Because that would leave her with
only me? Penny wondered, grinning. What a horrid
fate—for both of us!

But she herself knew she would kiss her sister on
her wedding day and wave good-bye to her with
never a single regret, although she was sure she
would miss her. And if it meant she had to live
alone in Northumberland with Aunt Eliza, well,
surely there were other things that were worse.
Like slavery, she thought gloomily. Or death.

The duke came in much later and challenged her
to some hands of piquet. He had been teaching her
that game for some time now, and Penny crowed
every time she won.

"Glad to see Phillipa has gone out with Deirdre
by herself," he said as he shuffled the cards.
"Something I should know about there?"

"Not yet, there isn't, sir," Penny said, with a
sunny smile. "But we shall see."

"I heard that Deirdre's cousin, Christopher
Blakely, has come to town," the duke remarked
next, carefully not looking at her as he dealt. "Nice
young man. Tragedy about his wife. The poor child
was not even twenty when she died. But he's a
solid fellow, well breeched and well connected. Be
good for Phillipa if she didn't mind taking on another woman's children."

Penny threw her hand down. "Is there anything
you don't know, uncle?" she demanded, looking exasperated.

The duke appeared to consider this question seriously. "Well," he said as he sorted his hand, "I've
never been able to understand how the new steam

engine works, or those devilish gaslights. But I cannot think of anything else."

"Sir, you are the most complete hand!" Penny said. As the duke looked askance, she added quickly, "Er . . . that is to say, you are certainly astute!"

"Pick up your cards, niece," he said, refusing the compliment.

Penny did learn about the outing from Deirdre when they met that evening at the Countess of Hasting's musical evening. Phillipa had declined to attend. Lady Eliza was having one of her headaches, and she claimed she needed her favorite niece beside her. Penny had been disappointed in her sister when she refused to go, but perhaps that was because she knew Mr. Blakely had not been included in the party, as Deirdre was quick to point out.

"It was beyond anything great!" she told Penny during one of the intermissions. "Phillipa looked so lovely in her pink muslin with that pretty bonnet—you know the one. And saintly with James in her arms. Fortunately, the motion of the carriage put him to sleep almost at once, so she could concentrate on looking angelic."

"Phil is never devious, Deirdre," Penny pointed out, frowning a little.

"I know she isn't. She doesn't have the brains for it," Deirdre said simply. Penny shook her head, but she hurried on, "And Chris! Well, he is too old to be obvious about it, but I could tell. I haven't seen him this taken with any woman since Helen's death. Of course, it's early days yet, but I do not repine. We may well have a happy ending."

"It was very good of you to do this for Phil," Penny said as she squeezed her hand. "You have been so kind to us both."

"Why, here is Mr. Whitaker!" Deirdre said brightly

as that gentleman bowed before them. Penny's heart sank. Was this to be the fatal time he would say something? Of course, if it were only to Deirdre, it would not matter, for she knew all about the adventure. But if he included others who were standing close by, it would be a mighty scandal. And that would put paid to all Phil's chances of marriage, her uncle's reputation ... Perhaps she should try and speak to him alone? Beg him to hold his tongue?

"You have met my cousin, Penelope Shaw, sir?" Deirdre asked him.

"Yes, at Mrs. Kincaid's the other evening. Servant, Miss Shaw."

Penny curtsied, giving him a pleading look as she did so. He seemed confused by it for a moment, although he hid it well.

"Oh, there is Sally Jersey. Do excuse me for a minute, Penny. I must tell her a delicious piece of gossip I heard recently."

Bartholomew Whitaker watched her flit across the room, his expression unreadable. "Ah, gossip! What would the ton do without it?" he murmured.

Although she was frightened that his words had hidden meaning, Penny decided to throw her heart over this particular fence, as she had so often, riding cross-country in Northumberland.

"Sir, may I speak to you a little apart?" she asked.

He held out his arm. "But of course. Shall we see if there are any ices left? I believe the dining room is almost empty."

Seated at a small table minutes later—one that was on the other side of the room from an amorous couple deep in whispered conversation—Whitaker looked at her and said, "Miss Shaw, it appears that you are frightened of me for some reason. I do assure you there is no need to be. I am not a malicious man, nor do I, like some others, relish scandal."

Penny's smile was warm and heartfelt, and his sleepy eyes opened a little. So, this was why Thornbury was so involved with the girl, was it? Her smile had the radiance of a thousand candles, and it transformed her.

"I am relieved to hear you say so, sir!" she said. "I have been so worried that you might tell everyone that you saw me that day in the carriage, with two men I am not related to, and nary a chaperon for miles. I know how it must have looked to you, but there is a simple explanation . . ."

He raised his hand. "It is not necessary that you tell me anything about it, however," he said.

"But I think you deserve to know, as payment for your kindness," Penny said, smiling still. "And really, it was just a silly mistake."

She skipped lightly over Alastair Pettibone's reason for abducting the lady who owned the scarlet cloak in her telling, leaving Whitaker with the impression it had all been a lark gone wrong. By the time she reached her night at the elderly Pettibones, and her subsequent flight to town, he was holding his sides and having trouble repressing gales of laughter.

"My compliments, ma'am," he said as he wiped his eyes. "You are truly unique!"

"No, I'm not," Penny said honestly. "I just seem to get into trouble more than most people. I don't know why. I don't go looking for it, you know."

"It just finds you?" he asked, already her slave. "Well, I shall be happy to assist you if you find yourself in any more.

"As for trouble, if we do not rejoin the others soon, you might find yourself deep in it even tonight. Shall we?"

Penny looked around. The amorous couple had

left, and only a few servants stood about waiting for them to leave, so they could finish clearing the tables. As Bartholomew Whitaker held out his arm, she rose quickly.

"I see Thornbury is not here tonight," she remarked as they went to the hall.

Ah, thought Whitaker, so that's what's what, is it? "No," he said aloud. "He is not fond of sopranos, and I am sure would have disgraced himself by fleeing during that last performance we heard."

"I thought it was only my lack of musical training that made me think her shrill," Penny admitted as they took seats at the back of the drawing room.

"I see we are to have a flutist now," he whispered.

"You are musical yourself, sir?" Penny asked him, her eyes twinkling.

He shook his head. "No, hate it. All of it. But Countess Hasting is a dear friend of my grandmother's. A *very* dear friend," he added gloomily. Penny giggled a little and then fell silent as an elderly dowager nearby gave her a repressive look.

Penny went to bed that night feeling much more lighthearted than she had for days. To think Mr. Whitaker would be so kind! What a very nice man he was! She would like to have him for a friend, she decided as she pulled up the covers and snuggled into her pillows. And he was so amusing, witty, and easy to talk to. Yes, a very nice man indeed. It occurred to her that he was much nicer than Laurence Russell, Marquess of Thornbury. Still, it was Thornbury she fell asleep thinking about, and wasn't that odd? She did not understand herself at all.

During the next week, Penny was glad to see her sister did not refuse to attend any of the events to which they were invited. There were afternoon teas, a silver loo party, an evening at the theater, and three soirees. Christopher Blakely attended most of these as well, and Penny was secretly elated when he came to Phillipa's side so often to talk to her, or ask her to dance. It seemed to Penny that Phillipa did not discourage his attentions, although she was still strangely reticent about him when the two sisters were alone together. Penny did not question her, although she often remarked how nice Mr. Blakely was, what a winning smile he had, how delightful a laugh. Phillipa always agreed and changed the subject, and with that, Penny had to be content.

She told herself she was glad that Phil was becoming more independent, even as she wished she knew what was going on in her pretty blond head.

Deirdre had her picnic at last, one warm spring day. The guests were summoned to her family home near Richmond, on the banks of the Thames.

Lady Clarissa Blakely welcomed them with a gracious smile. She was a comfortable, motherly woman, and if she had put on a lot of weight since her marriage, that could be attributed to the number of progeny she had presented her lord. Her home was a large, rambling structure with several wings, and it was surrounded by gardens and a maze for the guests to investigate. The maze was Lord Blakely's pride and joy, one he was constantly adding to, or revising, for he was determined it would be the most difficult in England.

By now, Penny knew most of the guests at the picnic, and she was not surprised to see Mr. Blakely coming to greet them. Somewhat beyond him, Laurence Russell stood with a group of gentlemen. He nodded to Penny, but his sober expression did not change. To repay him, she gave Bartholomew Whitaker her warmest smile.

Penny strolled with her sister and Mr. Blakely until she could decently make her escape by claiming she must go to Deirdre, saying she had promised to help her.

"Perhaps I should go with you?" Phillipa ventured to say.

Penny hid her annoyance. "Oh, no, dear. There is no need. I'll soon find you again."

With a whirl of white muslin skirts, she was away before Phil—who did not seem to have the least idea how to go on!—could insist.

Deirdre had everything well in hand, as Penny had known she would, but she stayed beside her for quite a while, then joined another group of people exploring the gardens.

Bartholomew Whitaker was quick to join her when the picnic was served. He filled a plate of delicacies for her before he took her to some benches set beneath a massive oak. Mr. Blakely, Phillipa, and some others came shortly thereafter.

Deirdre had provided a delicious repast. There were little biscuits filled with chicken or ham, salmon mousse, pâté and fresh fruit and cheese, and tarts containing the first strawberries. Servants passed among the guests pouring champagne.

"I am so full I may not move for the remainder of the afternoon," Penny declared as she put her fork down at last. "How good that was!"

"But you *must* move," Mr. Whitaker told her. "You have yet to see the maze, and Lord Blakely will be very disappointed if every single guest does not. And manage to get lost in it as well. I had the key memorized the last time I was here, but I understand he has added several fiendish new twists. It will be a challenge."

"We have never been in a maze, have we, Phil?" Penny asked. "What fun it will be!"

"But—but what if we get lost?" Phillipa whispered, looking frightened. "We might be in there for hours!"

"There is nothing to be afraid of," Christopher Blakely told her, patting her hand. "See there, Miss Shaw—that tall chair? A gardener sits there, so he can spot any lost, wandering souls when it grows late. You must let me take you through, for like Whitaker, I consider it a challenge. And just imagine how much fun Matthew and George must have when they visit their grandparents!"

Phillipa smiled at that, and Penny silently blessed Mr. Blakely for his talent at putting her sister at her ease.

But when she herself rose to go to the maze with Bartholomew Whitaker, they were joined by Thornbury. Penny wondered where he had been, for she had not seen him after that first, unsatisfactory glimpse. Had he been avoiding her? she wondered. But why?

"Ah, Miss Shaw. Going for a turn in the maze?"

Penny raised her chin. "As you say. Mr. Whitaker is going to take me."

"Indeed?" Thornbury asked, looking grim. "You must allow me to join you as well. Two heads . . . er . . . excuse me, Miss Shaw, *three* heads are better than one."

Seething, Penny could do nothing but nod. Who did this impossible creature think he was? she fumed as they walked over the velvet grass. She tilted her new parasol over her shoulder in a way that made it difficult for Thornbury to see more than her stubborn little chin, and gave most of her attention to Bartholomew Whitaker. To her chagrin, Whitaker seemed amused, and that did nothing for her temper.

Several others were already inside the maze when they arrived. They could hear their voices as they explored one avenue after another, laughing and chatting.

"No, I am sure we have been this way before, Sir Hevron," a young lady's voice exclaimed. "Don't you remember that monkey?"

"Sev-several of the bushes have been pruned into that shape," Sir Hevron protested. "I am sure I have nev-never seen that—that one before."

"Oh, dear! Another dead end!" said another laughing voice. "I fear we shall never escape!"

"Of course we shall, Margery. Tallyho, and all that!"

"It does sound formidable," Penny remarked, intrigued in spite of herself. "I can hardly wait to try it—and conquer it!"

"Forward!" Whitaker said, opening the wicker gate for her.

For some time they merely strolled through the maze, exploring it till they were deep inside. Several times they met others, flushed and excited, who assured them this was a puzzle that was impossible to decipher. Since the maze covered almost an acre of ground, Penny began to think them right.

"I could have sworn this path would lead us to the central fountain," Whitaker said, looking around the high-hedged alley that ended so abruptly in a cul-de-sac that contained a marble bench.

"Let us stop for a moment and think," Penny said, sinking down on the bench and waving her handkerchief before her flushed face. "Is it necessary to find the center before you get out, sir?"

"It was last year," Whitaker remarked. "Here, you rest for a while, Miss Shaw, while I try a different approach. I won't be gone long."

Penny wished she were not to be left alone with the strangely silent Thornbury, but Whitaker had disappeared before she could protest.

"I see you are enjoying the maze even though we may well be lost in it," the marquess remarked as he took a seat beside her.

"Of course I am," Penny said as lightly as she could. Why, oh, why did he have to sit so close to her? she wondered, hoping she was not blushing. She was much too aware of him—so tall and strong and masculine—next to her.

"I wonder if Bart has lost himself," he remarked in the little silence that ensued. "He does not appear to be coming back for us quickly. But of course . . ."

To his amazement, a small hand covered his mouth, and he looked at Penny Shaw, his dark brows raised. She shook her head at him, looking fierce, and raised her other hand to put a finger across her lips.

The two sat completely silent. Thornbury heard birds singing some distance away, and an occasional shout of laughter from other parts of the maze, and he wondered what had prompted her to such an unusual move.

"Oh, dear! We are truly lost!" a soft voice said from somewhere on the other side of the hedge.

"Is that such a bad thing, Miss Shaw?" a husky male voice asked. "Come, sit down over there on that bench and admire the fountain with me. It is lovely, is it not?"

"But I cannot see any gardener, or even his chair now," she said in a worried voice. "What if he cannot see us? How will we get out?"

"Why, I will shout at the top of my lungs. Do not concern yourself. And I am so delighted to have this time alone with you . . . Pippa."

The two voices grew fainter, and Thornbury told himself he was not a bit surprised when Miss Penny Shaw rose stealthily and moved closer to the hedge, parting it carefully and leaning forward, so she might eavesdrop further. How typical of her! he thought. Then he had to grin, for bent over, with her head and shoulders inside the foliage, she looked much like an ostrich he had seen once at the Royal Menagerie. Much prettier, though, he admitted, admiring her round little bottom.

When Bartholomew Whitaker returned minutes later, she was still there. He looked at Thornbury inquiringly.

"Miss Shaw is interested in a conversation taking place on the other side of the hedge," Thornbury murmured.

Whitaker grinned. "Instead of yours, m'lord? How lowering for you! But she is the most intrepid girl, is she not?"

"*Shhh!*" came a fierce whisper from the depths of the hedge.

"She is nothing but trouble," Thornbury said softly but forcefully. "Headstrong, opinionated, yet naive."

His friend hid a grin. It appeared Miss Shaw was leading the mighty Marquess of Thornbury a merry chase. That he had lived to see the day! It was wonderful!

When she withdrew her head at last, Penny found two pairs of masculine eyes regarding her seriously, and she flushed. "I do not generally do that, you know," she said, with dignity. "But it was my sister, and I—I was concerned for her. I would not like her to become hysterical because they had lost their way."

"She did not sound the least hysterical to me," Thornbury told her coldly as he rose and went to her to remove some twigs that had attached themselves to the curls peeping from her bonnet.

"Stand still!" he ordered. "You cannot return to the company looking like a hoyden!"

"Oh, surely a wood nymph, rather?" Whitaker

asked, swallowing his laughter. "Assure you, Miss Shaw, nothing of the hoyden about you."

"Isn't there just?" Thornbury demanded, taking her shoulders in his big hands and turning her this way and that in inspection.

Before Penny could give him a scathing set down for the liberty he took, he added, "And now shall we attempt to escape from this hot prison?"

It was true the hedges cut off whatever little breeze there was, and Penny could feel her shift sticking to her back.

"I did find the center," Whitaker told them. "Here, it is this way."

It was a long time before they found their way out of the maze, but Penny was glad they had not had to be rescued by the gardener. And to her relief, she saw Phillipa had left it as well, for she was down admiring the river, still escorted by Christopher Blakely. She had been able to hear very little of their quiet conversation through the hedge, but she was sure his continued interest was promising. And he *had* called her Pippa!

"I believe Lady Manning is signaling to you," Thornbury said. "Perhaps you had better see what she wants."

His voice was so cold, Penny stared at him in amazement, a little lump in her throat as she thanked them both, then ran away, all her pleasure at Phillipa's conquest gone in an instant.

Twelve

THE DUKE OF Longford was much occupied attending to the details of the ball he intended to give shortly. His task was complicated by the necessity of having to deal with servants upset by his sister's meddling. He had to countermand her orders for only the smallest supper, the fewest flowers, and the least amount of hired servants and catered items. But it was not until she told the orchestra he had engaged to play for dancing that only half their number would be sufficient that Longford called her into his study to ring a peal over her head.

"I tell you, Lizzy, I have had enough of your penny-pinching ways!" he said loudly, quite forgetting the butler and footmen in the hall outside.

"I was just trying to help you, William, and never did I think to hear such ingratitude," Lady Eliza said indignantly. "Like most men, you have no idea of economy, and—"

"The hell with economy!" he roared, and she cringed back in her seat, suddenly frightened. "This is *my* house, *my* money, and *my* ball! And you will not say another word about it! My housekeeper and butler have been planning my entertainments for years, and I will not have their arrangements overset. And the only person in this establishment to be consulted, is myself. *Do you understand?*"

"Certainly," she said in a tiny, weak voice, then she sniffed. The duke's heart did not soften, nor did he go to her and tell her he was sorry. She waited, but when nothing more was forthcoming, she added tartly, "If it were not for dearest Phillipa, I would go home tomorrow, for it is plain you do not want me here."

Exasperated, the duke ran a hand through his hair. "I am glad to have you visit, Lizzy, but I will not pretend that you're not enough to drive a saint to sin. As for your dearest Phillipa—and I notice Penny is not included in that category—I do not think you will have to worry about her much longer."

"What?" she demanded, sitting forward on her chair and fixing him with an awful eye. "Whatever do you mean?"

"I mean that much to my surprise, she is in the way of contracting a most eligible connection. It shall have my blessing, and as you know, I alone am named the girls' guardian."

His sister was holding her vinaigrette to her nose now for a deep sniff, and, uneasily, he wondered if he should have broken the news to her in quite such a way. He knew if he had not been so annoyed with her, he probably would have been more tactful.

"Who is this *eligible*?" Lizzy asked, her words dripping scorn. "Phillipa has said nothing to me of any man!"

"I daresay she sees how painful it will be for you," her brother said more kindly. "And there is no declaration made as yet, no call on me for permission to pay addresses. But Lizzy, it is time to let the girl go."

"Well, of course I hope dear Phillipa will marry someday, but only when she is less fragile, less timid and nervous."

"She will never become so, under your wing. You encourage her to coddle herself and start at every shadow. She is so different from Penny, I have often wondered how two sisters could have grown up so disparate."

"Oh, there is no mistaking your preference for Penelope! That madcap girl! I quite despair of *her* ever making any match, eligible or otherwise. Although, knowing Penelope as well as I do, I am sure if she did show a preference for anyone, he would be most unsuitable!"

"I doubt that. But never fear you will have her on your hands for long, Lizzy, for you are quite mistaken. Indeed, it is not too soon for you to consider where you want to live after the girls wed. I intend to sell their family estate and add it to their dowries. It is too far north, and too desolate, to make a pleasant country retreat. You think about it," he added, coming to help her to her feet and give her plump shoulders a brief hug. "I've a neat little place in Kent you could have, or perhaps you would prefer a house near Longford, where you grew up?"

Before she could reply, he added as they reached the library door, "You will not, however, bother Phillipa about any beau she might have, and you will not say one more word about this ball! That is an order! And Lizzy," he added as she began to open the door and make good her escape, "that includes trying to choose the girls' ensembles. Deirdre has excellent taste. They will look charmingly."

Deeply affronted, Lady Eliza sailed past him, and he shook his head as he went back to his desk.

Penny was preoccupied at dinner and did not notice her aunt's look of umbrage and long periods of silence, nor her sister's absentmindedness. Fortunately the duke was not averse to conducting a gentle monologue, although he wondered what the matter was with the girls. Thinking of their young men, no doubt, he thought, smiling to himself.

Penny was not doing any such thing. Rather, she was pondering a note she had had that afternoon from Louisa Bellings. It was a very proper note, begging her pardon for disturbing her, but requesting the return of her cloak in a way that seemed a thinly veiled threat. Penny did not know what to do. She did not like to bother her uncle with this when he was so busy with the ball. And certainly Phillipa would be no help. As for her aunt . . . No, no! That would never do!

I could ask Thornbury to call, she thought as she took a serving of sole in lemon sauce and some new peas. Ask him what I should do, even though I wish I did not have to after the way he treated me at the picnic.

She had inspected the scarlet cloak again that same afternoon. She had hidden it in an old trunk at the back of the box room. But although she spent some time looking it over, she could still see nothing unusual about it. She could not even feel anything concealed in it, for when she crushed it in her hands, there was no telltale rattle of paper.

Mrs. Bellings's note had instructed her to leave the cloak, well wrapped in brown paper, at a tavern in Hanstown, directed to a Mary Dodd, but she was loathe to do that.

Finally Penny decided that she had to ask Thornbury's advice. She would ask him to call here some time when she knew the duke would be out. And I am sure I can persuade Tuttle to let me see him alone, she thought. I know he has no love for my aunt, not after the way she has harried him about extravagance.

She began to eat her dinner with more appetite then, and by careful questioning, learned the duke intended to spend the morning at his club.

After dinner, she excused herself to write a quick note, which she entrusted to the butler. "Please send a footman with this at once, dear Mr. Tuttle," she begged, with a warm smile. "It is most urgent!"

Tuttle had seen the direction; he knew it was not at all the thing for young girls to correspond with a man, but somehow he found himself bowing and agreeing. Miss Penelope certainly has a way about her! he thought, shaking his head at both their folly.

The marquess received the note when he returned from an evening playing cards with friends. He frowned when he read the signature, and he was still frowning as he read her cryptic message. *What* matter of grave urgency? he wondered. *What* matter we have so often discussed? Intrigued, he gave his valet orders to wake him at eight and took himself off to bed.

By ten, Thornbury was being admitted to the Duke of Longford's house in Berkeley Square. He thought the butler looked very much the conspirator, and he wouldn't have been at all surprised to see the man wink at him as he escorted him to a small salon, closing the door carefully behind him. He was not left cooling his heels for long, for only minutes later, Penny Shaw slipped inside, looking anxiously over her shoulder.

"This is not at all the thing," he said as she shut the door. "Most irregular."

"I know, but I cannot be missish now," Penny said as she put a package she carried on a table nearby. "I have had a note from Louisa Bellings asking me to return her cloak. Ordinarily, I would do so in a moment, but something tells me it would be most unwise. An intuition, do you suppose, like you confessed you had now and then, m'lord? In any case, I thought to ask you what I should do."

"Why didn't you ask your uncle?" he said, staring at her coldly.

Penny seemed to realize that they were both still standing, and she said, "Oh, do sit down and take that stupid Friday face away! It is enough to give anyone the megrims!"

Startled, Thornbury did as he was told.

"My uncle knows nothing about the cloak—well, not as much as we do. He would probably advise me to return it."

"Is that it?" he asked, nodding toward the package.

"Yes, I brought it down. I have looked it over very carefully, but I could find nothing strange about it. Perhaps we have been wrong?"

"There's only one way to find out," he said, getting up to unwrap the package. Holding the cloak in his hands, he gave it a good shake.

"Do you have a pair of scissors, Miss Shaw?"

"You aren't going to destroy it, are you?" she whispered.

"I'll try not to. The scissors?"

"I thought you might need them, so I brought them with me," Penny said, reaching into the pocket of her morning gown.

Holding her breath, she watched the marquess as he ripped a seam open in the lining, then another, and another. She gasped when she saw the pocket, which had been sewn to the wrong side of the lining, and leaned closer as he carefully opened it. Inside was a thin package of silk.

It seemed to take forever before Thornbury had that package open, for he moved with great care now. Inside was a piece of hot-pressed paper, carefully folded, each fold encased in more silk.

"So that is why it did not rustle when I felt it!" she exclaimed, her eyes shining. "Oh, what does it say?"

To her disgust, Thornbury held the paper away from her to read it silently. As he did so, his face looked in turn astounded, disgusted, and finally, grim.

"Well?" Penny demanded, fuming with impatience.

"Better you do not know," he said, folding the paper and putting it in his notecase.

"Well, I like that!" she said indignantly. "How very unfair, when it was *I* who got the cloak in the first place! Besides . . ."

He stared at her, his eyes narrowed, and she fell silent. "I do assure you, you would not care to hear what is written there," he said, his voice constricted. "Or learn the writer's name, or the name of the person the letter was addressed to. I wonder how Alastair ever . . . But never mind that now," he added hastily.

"But you have to tell me *something*!" Penny insisted, coming to grasp his lapels as if to shake him in her frustration.

He stared at her hands for a moment before he reached up and gently removed them. "Weston would not approve any damage done to one of his creations, Miss Shaw," he said as Penny blushed. "But very well. I don't think it will do any harm to give you a general idea. I trust you can keep quiet about this?"

As she nodded, he went on, "The letter was written by a titled lady who is married to a most important man in government. It is written to her lover; in his own right, a prominent man. The letter makes it very clear the two have been lovers for a long time, both before and after their marriages to other people. And it reveals that the lady's firstborn son is not her husband's.

"If this ever came out, there would be a scandal

of the first water, for it involves a royal. The monarchy as we know it might well be destroyed.

"Women!" he said in disgust. "Only a woman would be so foolish as to put all that in writing! For you can see how easy it would be to blackmail her with it—or him. And I am sure that is what Louisa Bellings has planned. This letter is why she wants her cloak back so desperately.

"Tell me, how were you to get it to her? Did she give you an address?"

Penny shook her head. "I was to leave it at a tavern in Hanstown, care of a Mary Dodd. It is a poor place, that tavern, most unsavory."

"You have been there?" he demanded, frowning again.

"I had the coachman take me yesterday, after I received the letter," she admitted. "But I had two grooms with me, and I never went inside, so you need not look as black as thunder again!"

When he only continued to stare at her, she went on, "But what are we to do now? Even if I sew the cloak back together, Mrs. Bellings will know I have found her out when she opens it and discovers the letter gone. And she might well want revenge on me. I—I do not think she is a nice person."

"On that point we are in complete agreement. No, you must not return that cloak."

He rose then to pace up and down, caressing his jaw in that familiar gesture. At last he said, "Do nothing for a while. I have a man searching for Mrs. Bellings, and surely he will discover where she is living soon. Then I shall call on her myself and let her know her nefarious scheme is discovered. Perhaps I shall even issue a few threats of my own."

"It is very good of you, m'lord," Penny said, her voice wooden.

He came to stand close to her, taking her chin in

his hand. "Why do you sound that way?" he asked, his voice curiously gentle.

Penny's face paled so that every one of the little freckles on the bridge of her nose stood out in bold relief. "It doesn't seem at all fair to me!" she said in a rush. "You are going to have all the adventure, when it was *my* adventure all along!"

He grimaced and released her. As he picked up the cloak and wrapped it in the paper again, he said, "Then I'd better take this along with me, lest you see yourself as the heroine of the piece and take it to Hanstown yourself, no matter how you have been warned against such a thing. Give you good day, Miss Shaw."

Penny stared at the door he closed softly behind him. She felt absolutely miserable, but although she tried to tell herself that was only because she had been deprived of any future role in the matter of Louisa Bellings's cloak, she had to admit it was really because of the way Thornbury was treating her. How angry he had looked his morning! How severe!

The man she was thinking of went immediately to his cousin's rooms near Jermyn Street. He was on foot, and he little cared for the stares he received from the elite who saw him striding along carrying a large parcel wrapped in brown paper. To say he was furious, was to put it mildly. He did not know how Alastair had come into possession of that damning letter, but he intended to find out. This time he has gone too far! Thornbury told himself as he knocked at last on his cousin's door. For even if he had come by the letter innocently, which he found hard to believe, he had certainly intended to make mischief with it. Thornbury had never thought Alastair Pettibone an evil man, only a weak, lazy one who would always look for the easiest way. But perhaps he had been mistaken in his judgment of him?

Pettibone's valet admitted him, telling him Mr. Alastair was still at breakfast. When he offered to take the parcel, he was curtly refused.

Thornbury found his cousin at a table in his sitting room, reading his post and enjoying a second cup of coffee. He was wearing a dressing gown over his shirt and breeches, and any other time, the marquess would have laughed out loud, for it was a violent paisley of violet, gold, and green that resembled a multitude of writhing snakes. Today, however, he only gave it a cursory glance as he shut the door in the valet's face.

"Cuz! What brings you here, looking so black?" Pettibone asked nervously.

"I understand you have been making inquiries about Louisa Bellings's cloak," Thornbury said as he stripped off his gloves and took a seat at the table. "Since it is so important to you, I have brought it with me."

"That is the cloak?" Pettibone whispered, his eyes lighting up.

Thornbury unwrapped the parcel and handed his cousin the mutilated garment.

"But—but it has been ripped open!"

"Unfortunately, I cannot give you the letter that was hidden in it," Thornbury said coldly. "But now, Alastair, you will tell me how you got that letter, and what you intended to do with it."

"I—I don't know what you mean . . ."

"Don't play games with me!" Thornbury shouted, striking the table with his clenched fist. The dishes on it clattered, and his cousin jumped.

"Very well, if you insist! I know you will find it hard to believe, but I chanced upon it quite by accident. No," he added, waving his hand, "do not look at me so, like a devil! It *was* by accident. I'd been down to the Foreign Office to see Tom Dickson, and as I was leaving, I saw this paper lying in the corridor. The man it belonged to must have dropped it there. Or perhaps it fell out of his notecase."

"Indeed?" Thornbury asked scornfully. "That seems rather careless of him, don't you think? A letter of that magnitude, one that could bring about his downfall and his mistress's, to say nothing of the government, and he dropped it?"

"He must have," Pettibone said stubbornly. "I remember the place was bustling that day. Something to do with the French, of course, and war plans. Many people were carrying papers here and there. Even Tom had little time for me.

"But it's true, Laurence! It was lying on the floor and I—I just picked it up."

"But you didn't return it, did you, although his name was written plainly? Nor did you destroy it. You put it away in your own notecase, did you not? For what reason?"

Pettibone wiped his forehead on his napkin. "I don't know. I wasn't going to bring about a scandal, if that's what you are implying. I just thought it would be amusing to keep it."

"Did you indeed? Are you sure you did not think to try a little blackmail yourself?"

Pettibone rose so rapidly, his chair fell over. "How dare you?" he asked through white lips. "How dare you even suggest such a thing?"

The marquess leaned back at his ease, but his dark eyes never left his cousin's face. "Probably because I know the state of your finances, cuz. You are on the brink of ruin, with no way out. I have been waiting for you to hit bottom and come to me for aid. When this letter fell into your hands so fortuitously, surely the idea you could not only make a recovery but a possible fortune with it must have occurred to you."

"Well, it did, but I knew it was not at all the thing," Pettibone muttered as he ran an agitated hand through his hair.

"How did Louisa Bellings get her hands on it? It seems to me you must have been as careless with it as its original owner."

"She stole it, of course—the witch! I had it safely tucked away in my own notecase, but she must have searched for it while I was sleeping."

"Did she often make a practice of going through your things, or had you told her of it? But of course you did! You have never been able to keep a tasty little bit of gossip to yourself, have you, cuz? I can almost hear you crowing about it to her!"

Pettibone flushed. "I never mentioned any names," he said, defending himself from the scorn written so plainly on Thornbury's face. "I just gave her a few hints, y'know. Nothing at all specific."

"Specific enough for her to know how valuable it was. Of course she intended to blackmail him. Or her."

"I've no idea what she planned. When I woke, she was gone, bag and baggage, and I've not seen her from that day to this. That was why I was searching for her, you see. I had to get that letter back before she made a scandal. I have been frantic. Of course, when there was no scandal, and she made such a to-do about her missing cloak, I assumed she had hidden the letter in it somehow for safekeeping. I suppose I must be grateful to you for locating it, for now we may all be easy."

"Oh, I doubt you will find your future lot *easy*," Thornbury told him as he wrapped the cloak up again. "You see, Alastair, I rather feel the family will be much better off if you are not seen in England for quite a long time. As you know, I have a sugar plantation in Jamaica. The overseer needs assistance. You will provide that assistance. I expect you to leave on the next ship sailing to Kingston."

"Damn it! You can't make me go!" Pettibone exclaimed. "You may be the head of the family, but you can't order me about!"

Thornbury strolled to the door. "Can't I?" he asked coolly. "If you refuse, I shall simply see that the tale of your infamy is known throughout the ton. Oh, yes, I will sacrifice our name gladly in this case. In a short time, no one will receive you. It won't matter how many little tidbits you can glean, for no one will be speaking to you. The rest of us will muddle through somehow. Every family has its dirty dishes."

"Laurence, don't do this!" Pettibone begged, his shoulders sagging. "I beg you, don't!"

"You have been a thorn in my flesh for years, cuz. I'm tired of it. Perhaps a few years of honest toil, early rising, and no gambling will make a man of you. We shall have to see."

He opened the door then, and Alastair's valet stumbled away. "I suggest you look about for a new position, sir," Thornbury told him. "Where your master is going, he will not need your services. And Alastair," he added, turning to his cousin again, "I will send you your passage money and enough to pay your debts. If reports from my overseer are glowing enough, there will be more. Who knows? I may even relent eventually and allow you to return. Safe voyage."

When he reached home in Pall Mall, Thornbury did four things. First, he instructed his butler to have the scarlet cloak destroyed. Secondly he wrote a short note to the owner of the letter, telling him that he had come upon it by chance and destroyed it. He and his mistress were safe. Thirdly he took the letter from his notecase and put it in the empty fireplace grate and lit it. He did not take his eyes from it until it was nothing but gray ash. Only then did he smile a little in relief. The last thing he did was to send a message to his man, Sam Bottoms, alerting him to the tavern in Hanstown where Louisa Bellings was sure to call. Bottoms was to follow her when she left the place, discover where she was staying.

For the remainder of the day, he found himself thinking of Penny Shaw and wondering what he was to do about her. She was still in danger, for when the Bellings woman did not get her cloak back, who knew what vengeance she might exact in her disappointment? Somehow Penny must be kept safe, no matter how tame she would consider that!

He reviewed his engagements. Yes, the next time he could be sure of seeing her was at the ball her uncle was giving for her sister. That was in two days' time. He did not think Louisa Bellings would act before then. She might, however, write another letter to Penny. He must remember to ask her about that at the ball. And if necessary, he would consult the duke—ask him to send Penny out of town for a while. For nothing must happen to the girl, he told himself. Nothing!

Thirteen

THAT SAME MORNING, Phillipa Shaw ran her sister to earth in the small salon where Thornbury had left her. "Why, Penny! What are you doing in here all by yourself? It is not a bit like you," she said as she came in. She was dressed for the street in a light pelisse and truly becoming bonnet, and Penny forced herself to smile.

"I was just thinking about something," she admitted, then added quickly, "You look very nice. Where are you off to?"

Phillipa pretended fascination with one of the buttons on her glove. "Deirdre has kindly invited me to nuncheon. And after it, I am taking Matthew and George to see the sights. I promised to treat them to ices at Gunter's as well."

Wondering if Christopher Blakely was included in this outing, and reminding herself she must not ask, Penny only said, "You are much too good to those two scamps, Phil!"

"They are not scamps!" her sister said hotly. "Well, perhaps George is sometimes . . . But you must admit, Matthew is the perfect little gentleman."

"Yes, Deirdre is worried about him. But do run along and have a fine time."

"Penny, I wanted to ask you to go to Aunt Eliza. She has been so gloomy this morning, I scarce know what to think might ail her."

"And you imagine my attentions will cheer her up? You're all about in your head!" Penny said tartly. "But never mind. I'll see what I can do."

Her mind relieved of worry about her aunt, Phillipa was left at Lady Manning's door a short time later for a delicious nuncheon. She and Lord and Lady Manning were joined by Christopher Blakely, as had been arranged.

As he and Phillipa were standing in the hall later, waiting for the boys, Deirdre said, "It is very good of you to take the children this afternoon. I know Robert worries about them when we are in London, for he is a great believer in fresh air and exercise. And there's no denying the boys can't run about and play in town as they do at home."

"We will not bring them back until they are suitably exhausted," Blakely told her.

"I hope George will not be frightened by the wild animals at the Exeter 'Change," Phillipa said, frowning a little. "I told Mr. Blakely it might be too much for a child of three, but . . ."

"George frightened? Of anything?" Deirdre asked in amazement. "No, no! Just be sure he does not try to pet the tigers. I would not put it past him to attempt something of the sort."

Her cousin Christopher laughed as the boys came tumbling down the stairs, both talking at once.

The afternoon was such a success, that after treating their charges to ices at Gunter's, they took them into the enclosed park in the middle of Berkeley Square. Blakely seated Phillipa on a bench and waved the boys off to explore.

"Do you think we should let them go alone?" Phillipa asked, a little frown creasing her brow.

"They can come to no harm here, surrounded by these iron palings," he told her, patting her hand. "And I would like to talk to you alone . . . Pippa."

"I do not think you should call me that, sir," she said softly.

He captured her hand in his. "No, perhaps not, but I cannot help myself." He sighed then and released her. "It was fun this afternoon, was it not? You are so good with the children, and you seemed to enjoy it as much as they did."

"Oh, I did," Phillipa told him, raising glowing eyes to his. "Of course I thought the tiger frightful, but I tried not to show it, lest the children catch my fear."

"We must hope neither the tiger nor those two ices apiece you let them have will cause bad dreams tonight," he said, with a grin. "I fear you have too soft a heart, Pip—Miss Shaw."

He stared down into her lovely face, admiring her blue eyes and the roses in her cheeks. Phillipa stared back at him.

With an effort, she looked away. It was not at all the thing to be gazing so raptly at any gentleman, and she knew it. And who knew who might be watching her? Perhaps even Aunt Eliza from the windows of the duke's house across the square.

Suddenly she gave a little cry and rose to run as fast as she could to the far corner of the park.

"Pippa! What is it?" Blakely called after her as he started to follow her.

He saw she was making for a stranger who held George in his arms as he headed for one of the gates. Even as he quickened his pace, he wondered that George would go with a stranger so meekly.

"Cousin Chris, Cousin Chris!" Matthew panted, grabbing his coattail and slowing him considerably. "That bad man! He's got George!"

"I know. Let me go now so I can stop him. You wait right here," he ordered, his eyes never leaving Phillipa's slim form as she reached the stranger and grasped his arm.

"Stop at once!" he heard her cry. "Where do you think you are taking that child?"

The stranger did not answer as he tried to pull away from her. Blakely could see how George's head lolled against his shoulder, and he felt a sense of dread. What had he done to him?

The stranger was fighting off Phillipa with a vengeance now, but she did not release her hold on him. Two other women standing a little way from them went to her aid just as Blakely reached her side.

He saw Phillipa had hold of George now, trying to wrest him from the stranger's grasp. The man, who was dressed poorly, and of a slight build, saw the murder in Blakely's eyes and let George go. Just before Blakely could hit him, he pushed both Phillipa and the child toward him and fled.

Blakely was aware of the excited chatter of the onlookers, but all the noise they made faded from his ears as he caught Phillipa tight in his arms, holding her as if he never meant to let her go. The light lavender perfume she wore made him heady.

"George, you are safe now," she was saying as she smoothed the little boy's hair from his brow. "George? Why don't you speak to me?"

Blakely forced himself to forget how she felt in his arms and bent closer to the child. The faint, sweet smell of a drug lingered, and he frowned and looked wildly around, but the man who had tried to take George had disappeared.

"He has been drugged, my dear. Best we get him home and under a doctor's care as soon as possible. Matthew? Come here!"

The other boy ran to them, his face drawn with anxiety, and Christopher Blakely made himself smile. "No need to worry, old man. George is just having a little nap. But I think we'll leave now. Come along."

He gently transferred George to his own arms and bade Phillipa take Matthew's hand before he led them to his waiting carriage.

Nothing was said on their journey through the busy streets, and although Matthew had a hundred questions, somehow he did not like to voice them.

Once inside the Manning establishment, all was pandemonium for a while. Robert Shaw set a footman running for the doctor while his wife and the nursemaids took George upstairs to undress him and put him to bed. Matthew tagged along, anxious to tell his mother of the frightful experience they had had.

"Come into the library and have some wine, Phillipa, Chris," Robert Shaw invited. "You look like you could use it, and I would hear more of this."

The tale was soon told to a grim-faced, attentive father.

"So, you think it was a kidnapping attempt?" he asked, looking from one to the other.

"Yes, and one that might well have succeeded, had not Phillipa seen what he was up to—and rushed to prevent him leaving the park. She held him until I could get there. When he saw me, he decided to make a bolt for it."

To Phillipa's great embarrassment, the viscount got up and came to give her a hearty hug and a kiss. "Thank you," he said simply, not trying to hide the moisture in his eyes. "If anything had happened to George— But we are forever in your debt, Phillipa."

A short time later, after she had learned that George had taken no harm from the drugging, Phillipa was able to make her escape. Christopher Blakely insisted on taking her home himself.

She leaned back against the squabs of the carriage and sighed.

"You must be exhausted," Blakely said from his place by the opposite window.

"I am tired. The excitement, I guess, and the worry," she admitted. "But I am so glad George is all right. What I don't understand is why anyone would want to kidnap him."

"Shaw is a rich man, is he not? And his father, the duke, is even richer," Blakely told her.

He sounded abstracted, and Phillipa wondered why. And she wished he would not stare at her so! It was unnerving.

"Yes, I suppose that must have been the reason," she made herself say. "How horrid people are, to do such a thing to a little child!"

When the carriage pulled up before the duke's house, Phillipa looked at the park in the center of the square. It was peaceful now, but still she shuddered. Blakely saw it, and hugged her to him briefly as he helped her up the steps. Before he sounded the knocker, he took her gloved hand in his and kissed it in tribute.

"I shall call tomorrow to see how you go on, Miss Shaw," he said. "I want very much to talk to you, but I will wait. You are too tired now. Go inside and rest, and try to forget this afternoon. Will you do that for me?"

Phillipa nodded as she gently freed her hand from his clasp. The light she saw shining in his eyes made her feel not only unnerved, but breathless as well, and she sensed it was going to seem a very long time before tomorrow came.

Indeed, the hours passed slowly for Phillipa. She said nothing of the thwarted kidnapping attempt, or little George's drugging, for she did not want to call attention to herself.

Of course Penny heard all about it when she visited Deirdre the next morning. She was shocked, then amazed when she learned what a heroine her timid sister had been.

"I take back everything I have thought of Phillipa," Deirdre said earnestly. "But whoever would have imagined *she* could be so brave?"

"Not I," Penny assured her. "Of course, there is her love of children. I daresay she didn't even think of danger when she went to George's aid. He is all right?"

Deirdre chuckled a little. "Completely recovered, and very cock of the walk, I do assure you. Robert has hired a guard, not caring to entrust the boys' welfare even to a footman's care." She shivered. "How frightening it is, Penny, when your family is threatened. I could hardly sleep last night, and Robert—well! I have never seen him so grim. He looks like he would like to take us all to some impregnable castle with a moat around it."

"Does Uncle William know?"

"No. We decided it would only upset him. But no doubt he will learn of it one of these days . . ."

Unbeknownst to either Deirdre or Penny, the duke was learning of it that very moment. Christopher Blakely had called, asking to see him. And in the course of begging permission to pay his addresses to Phillipa, he had revealed the kidnapping plot and her success in foiling it.

"Phillipa did that?" Duke Longford asked, amazed. "Mistress Frightened?"

Blakely frowned. "She was not frightened then, sir. She was magnificent! It was then that I realized how much I loved her."

The duke rose, smiling. "Then I suggest you go and tell her so. I'll have Tuttle bring her to you," he said. "You are a good man, Blakely. You have my blessing."

As the two men walked to the library door, he

added, "And now, perhaps, we shall have a truly festive reason for my ball, eh, my boy?"

Christopher Blakely paced up and down a small salon for some time before Phillipa came to him. She had been much involved with her aunt that morning, and had yet to don more than a simple old morning gown. And, she told herself as she sped to her room, I will not meet Christopher looking like this!

As she changed, she pondered the confusing conversation she had just had with Lady Eliza. Her aunt had mentioned Phillipa's marriage "sometime in the future," saying she hoped her niece would not make a mistake by rushing into anything; advised her to be prudent and thoughtful; reminded her of her delicate emotional health. Phillipa had made soothing sounds and nodded frequently, but she did not understand Aunt Eliza at all.

When Christopher Blakely turned, he saw her standing at the salon door, blushing a little and looking thoroughly adorable to his besotted eyes.

"Pippa," he said, coming to draw her inside the room, then shutting the door behind them. She looked at him askance, and he said, "It is all right. Your uncle has given me permission to see you privately. Oh, Pippa . . ."

They stared at each other for a moment, then he put his arms around her and drew her close. Putting his cheek against her hair, he said huskily, "I know this is not the correct way to go about a proposal, but I can't help myself. Darling Pippa, I love you so much! Will you marry me?"

She drew back then, so she could study his face. "Do you mean it, Christopher?" she whispered.

"It is the wish of my heart, dearest. Will you? Say yes, Pippa, say yes!"

It seemed an endless time before she nodded shyly. At that he forgot all his resolutions to treat her gently, and he kissed her with all a man's deep yearning.

"Do you know, I was afraid to ask you before this, even though I fell in love with you at first meeting," he said several minutes later. "You see, I thought marriage would be too much for someone like you. You seemed so fragile to me, so nervous and sensitive. And I am a man, Pippa. I want all there is to marriage."

"Of course you do," she agreed, smiling a little. "And I know marriage will not be too much for me. Far from it!"

The evening of the duke's ball was not as fine as he would have wished. A misty rain had fallen all day, making it necessary for the footmen to arm themselves with umbrellas to escort the guests from their carriages to the mansion. But once inside, the inclement weather ceased to matter.

Of course the ball was a perfect crush. The ton revered William Shaw, and it knew from past experience that the evening would be special. The Marquess of Thornbury looked around in approval as he entered the ballroom. He had never seen it looking so well. The prisms of the chandeliers had been polished till they gleamed like diamonds, and large urns full of lush flowers from the Longford succession house decorated every table.

Surprisingly, he thought, Phillipa Shaw did justice to her surroundings. She was radiant tonight in a white silk gown, and she wore a pearl necklet that was especially fine, a gift from her uncle to mark the occasion. But it was her sister, Penelope, who drew his eyes almost at once. She was also wearing pearls. So much for not coming out! he thought with a wry smile, admiring her blazing curls.

He noticed she was seated beside an older

woman resplendent in purple, who looked at the proceedings with a jaundiced eye. Must be the "mean old bit" the tavern owner had mentioned, he told himself as he went to greet some of his friends.

The duke opened the ball with a blushing Phillipa Shaw, but he was quick to give her hand to Christopher Blakely.

"Have you heard?" Bartholomew Whitaker murmured behind him. "Miss Shaw is to marry Blakely. It has just been arranged. I wonder how long it will be before her sister follows her example . . . ?"

Thornbury turned and stared at him. "Surely you jest, Bart. She is nothing but a madcap child!"

"In years, perhaps," Whitaker agreed. "In other ways, she is as old as Eve."

When Thornbury looked astounded, he grinned. "I admire her a great deal," he said. "She has such a valiant heart. Don't you think so, sir?"

It was some time later before Laurence Russell could have a few minutes alone with Penny Shaw. At first, she had been much sought after as a partner by the younger beaux. Later she had been busy with her aunt and other relatives. But fortunately he was close by when the elderly Pettibones of Milfield arrived on the scene.

"There she is, Winston!" Elizabeth Pettibone said shrilly. "There is Miss Smith!"

"Mischief? Mischief? Where?" her husband demanded, raising his pince-nez for a thorough inspection of the room.

Thornbury saw Duke Longford was looking amused, and he hurried to join his eccentric relatives.

"Laurence, tell me my eyes do not deceive me!" Mrs. Pettibone demanded. "But I cannot be mistaken in that hair! That is Miss Abby Smith, is it not? The gel who ran away from you and Alastair?"

"No, no. You are wrong, ma'am," he said in a soothing voice, although he noted several people nearby were listening avidly. "That is Miss Penelope Shaw. She is Duke Longford's niece."

"Well, it's all of a piece to me," Mr. Pettibone said heartily. "Come along, Elizabeth. Must meet the duke. Kind of him to invite us to the ball."

"But I don't want to go to the hall," his wife complained. "We just got here."

Thornbury was relieved when she went with her husband nevertheless.

"Lordy, lordy," Penny muttered as he joined her. "I could just kill Uncle William! He never even warned me the Pettibones would be here! What am I to do?"

"To-do? To-do?" Thornbury asked, his dark eyes smiling down at her as he imitated his relatives. To his delight, Penny lost her worried look and gurgled with laughter.

"Come with me," he said, offering her his arm. "I want to talk to you."

Eager to escape the room that held her earlier chaperons, Penny was glad to agree. The two went into the portrait gallery. Several other people were there admiring the oils, but Thornbury managed to find a vacant sofa against the far wall.

"Have you heard from Louisa Bellings again, Miss Shaw?" he asked as soon as they were seated.

She frowned. "No, not a word. It occurred to me that it might be wise for me to write to her, tell her something that would explain why I have not returned her cloak. The problem is, I cannot think of anything to say."

"Do nothing yet. I imagine you will hear from her shortly, and I'd know of it when you do, if you please.

184

"Incidentally, she has not gone to that tavern in Hanstown as yet. I have been having it watched."

He saw Penny looked concerned still, and he added, "There is something else bothering you?"

"Yes. Deirdre's little boy was almost kidnapped the other day. If it had not been for my sister, he would have been taken right from the park outside this house. The man drugged him, you see, so he could not cry out. And ever since I learned of it, I have not been able to stop thinking that that might have happened because of the missing cloak."

She thought Thornbury looked dubious, and she said passionately, "No, listen to me! First there was that kitchen maid in my room, going through my clothes. That night we had the housebreaker, and Betty, the maid, disappeared the next day. Then Mrs. Bellings's note arrived. When I did not return the cloak, someone tried to kidnap George. I don't know much about London, but although I have heard what a wicked city it is, I do not think such things happen with such regularity, and to one family, too. It is too much a coincidence."

"You are right," he said slowly. "It is unusual. I did not know of the kidnapping. The Mannings must have been distraught."

He turned toward her then to take both her hands in his. "Now you will listen to me, Miss Penny Shaw. I believe you to be in great danger, and I warn you that you must be very careful."

Penny stared into his grim face as his hands tightened on hers. "Why would you care about that?" she asked, curious as to his reasons.

He did not look away. "Because it was my cousin's fault that you became involved in all this in the first place," he said easily. "I feel responsible."

"Oh," Penny said, hiding her disappointment.

"You will be interested to know that Alastair is about to embark on a journey to Jamaica and will be gone for some years," he said next, happy for some reason to change the subject.

"Now why do I get the distinct impression that you had something to do with his decision to travel?" Penny asked, head tipped to one side as she considered it. Then she said, "What happened to that letter we found in the cloak?"

"I destroyed it, after telling its owner I was going to do so. I am sure after he received my note, the man had a good night's sleep for the first time in weeks."

"So there will be no scandal. That is good. Still, I think it is shameful that such things happen. I mean that married people take lovers. It is very immoral of them."

"Do you feel they should be punished for it, forced to face a scandal?"

"I suppose we must leave them to heaven, as the Bible tells us. But I could never do such a thing, never!"

Thornbury smiled a little. How fierce she sounded! Yet looking into her honest blue eyes, he knew she spoke the truth. He was surprised to find himself wondering what it would be like to be loved by her, and, uncomfortable with the thought, he looked around.

He saw two of London's most accomplished quizzes were regarding them from across the gallery and whispering behind their fans. At once, he dropped Penny's hands, wondering why he had not realized he was holding them all this time.

Rising, he asked, "Shall we, Miss Shaw?"

As she obeyed, he added, "But remember what I have told you. Be careful. Do not go anywhere alone, for any reason, no matter how desperate you might consider the circumstances!"

"I wonder you don't just pat me on the head and tell me I must not talk to strangers, there's a good little girl!" she muttered in exasperation. "You will keep treating me like a child, m'lord, when I am no such thing!"

Thornbury kept his eyes on her face, carefully avoiding all the soft curves that were so artfully displayed in her gown of violet silk. "I agree you are not, but you are not mature as yet, either. Nor, from what I have seen of you, are you very wise."

Penny put up her chin, wielding her fan before her face, so she would not hit him with it as she longed to do. "That is only your opinion, m'lord," she said grandly.

"Please excuse me now," she added. "My aunt will be wondering what has become of me."

She was gone before Thornbury could reply. He smiled a little to himself, ruefully shaking his head until he remembered the two quizzes. As he left the room, he sported a most solemn expression.

Fourteen

WITH THE EXCEPTION of the servants, everyone in the Duke of Longford's mansion in Berkeley Square slept very late the day after the ball, for it had gone on almost till dawn. Penny had been amazed when three o'clock came and went, and people were still dancing, eating, drinking, and circulating through all the elaborate rooms of her uncle's house. And although she still considered the ton like a gaggle of silly geese, she did have to admit that if the people who comprised it had nothing else, they certainly did have stamina!

Penny had not spent any more time with Laurence Russell, and although a part of her regretted that, she told herself it was probably just as well. The man was infuriating! And when she was with him, she had to keep herself under firm control, lest she succumb to a violent urge to attack him.

William Shaw and Penny were the first to reach the breakfast room that morning, and they had barely finished their repast when Viscountess Manning was announced.

"You wanted to see me, sir?" she asked as she took a chair beside him and nodded as Penny indicated the teapot.

"I have learned of George's foiled kidnapping, Deirdre," he said stiffly. "And I must tell you I take umbrage that I did not hear of it from you or Robert. No, I must thank Mr. Blakely for keeping me informed about such a serious *family* matter. Well, what do you have to say for yourself, girl?"

He sounded so stiff and offended Penny stole a cautious look at him and shivered a little. She had never heard him speak so harshly, nor look so stern.

Deirdre reached over to take his hand in both of hers. "Dear sir, I know we have been at fault. But we did not want to upset you on the eve of your ball. And—"

"The ball be hanged!" he interrupted, not a bit mollified by this consideration. "I must remind you, George is my beloved grandchild! I had a right to know!"

"Well, you know now," Deirdre said calmly. "In fact, Robert intends to call on you today, to ask your advice. He is beside himself with worry for all of us. I hope you can ease his mind, sir, for there is no one he listens to—or reveres—more."

"Stop gammoning me!" the duke exclaimed. "Of course Robert and I will put our heads together, whenever he likes. Has he considered sending you all back to the country?"

Deirdre made a face. "Indeed he has. Of course, even though I would miss being here for the rest of the Season, I would go in a minute for my children's safety. But now we have a guard for them, and they are so carefully watched, I do not see the need."

The duke stared past her to the small garden outside the windows. Some early flowers were blooming there in the sunlight, not that he appeared to see them.

"No, perhaps that is not necessary," he said slowly. "But we have come to a sorry pass here in London, have we not? The criminal elements grow too bold, robbing and killing—and kidnapping small children for gain! We must have a metropolitan police force, and at once! The criminals must be stopped!"

His voice had risen till he was almost shouting, and his face was very red with his emotion.

"Sir! I quite agree a police force is necessary, but it cannot be good for you to become so angry," Deirdre said, her voice worried.

He smiled a little, looking from Deirdre's to Penny's concerned faces. "I know," he said more temperately. "But trust me to see Dr. Colquhoun or the Reverend Mr. Bentham who started the Thames Marine Police Force at Wapping. They will have some ideas how a city force might be formed and made effective. The Bow Street Runners and the Charlies are not enough, not anymore.

"Did you have a good time at the ball, Deirdre?" he asked next, abandoning a subject that he, courtly old gentleman that he was, did not consider suitable for ladies.

"I, and everyone else," she said, smiling now. "You do give the most lavish parties, sir."

"I know. Lizzy hasn't spoken to me for days," he said as he wiped his mouth and rose to excuse himself.

Phillipa came in to the breakfast room minutes later. Her eyes were a little heavy, but she still glowed with happiness.

"Ah, to be newly in love!" Deirdre teased her. "You seemed to have a wonderful time last evening, Phillipa, did you not? And when I think how I used to despair of ever making you easy in company!"

"I would not have been if Christopher had not been beside me," Phillipa told her as she spread jam on her scone. "But it is so different now. So much more comfortable."

The three talked for a while of the coming wedding, Deirdre promising to help Phillipa select her bride clothes.

Penny noticed her sister's little frown then, and asked what was troubling her.

"It is Aunt Eliza," Phillipa admitted. "She was so unhappy when she learned I was promised to Christopher. And although I think she is beginning to resign herself to it, now she has begun to talk of living with us."

"Oh, no!" both Deirdre and Penny exclaimed in unison.

They sounded so horrified, Phillipa had to smile a little. "I agree it is not what I would choose, but still, I feel guilty. She did raise us, Penny, and we owe her a great deal. And I do love her. It is just that, well . . ."

"You need not say another thing!" Deirdre told her. "The very idea! A bride and groom deserve to be alone together."

"That is what Christopher says," Phillipa admitted, blushing now. "In fact, he was most determined it would be so. He told me there was no way on earth he would agree to have Aunt Eliza live with us, and I must choose between them. How silly of him that ultimatum was! As if there was a chance I would choose aunt when I love him so! But still," she added pensively, "I do worry about her. Uncle William told me he plans to sell our place in Northumberland, for he intends for you to make your home with him from now on, Penny. But he has offered aunt a choice of houses in Kent or near Longford."

"Then she can go to either," Penny said, trying to hide the joy she felt that she was escaping her aunt's penny-pinching, disapproving chaperonage at last. How kind of the duke! She knew she would enjoy his company tremendously.

"She'll come around," Deirdre said as she collected her reticule and smoothed her gloves. "But you must be firm, Phillipa. Do not leave any doubt in her mind that your decision is a final one. Naturally you can mention her visiting you, sometime in the future. That will cheer her up. Just be sure not to say *when* in the future."

After Deirdre had gone, the two sisters sat on at the table, although Penny soon wearied of listening to yet another monologue about Christopher Blakely's marvelous qualities—his kindness, his good looks, his charming smile, his . . .

She was not at all sorry when Tuttle came in with a note for her, which had just been delivered. But when she glanced at it and recognized Louisa Bellings's handwriting, she excused herself at once. Better not to read it in Phillipa's company, she thought as she hurried to her room, shut the door, and broke the seal.

"Miss Shaw," the note began abruptly. "If my cloak is not delivered to the tavern in Hanstown, care of Miss Mary Dodd, by five o'clock this afternoon, you will be very sorry. There are so many unpleasant things that can happen, and not just to you, either. I read that your sweet sister is to be married. How tragic it would be if she came to grief! Or there is your old uncle, the duke, and his London house. Fire can cause so many tragedies.

My cloak, Miss Shaw. Today."

The letter was not signed. There was no need.

Penny's face was so pale when she finished reading, the tiny golden freckles on the bridge of her nose stood out in bold relief. What am I to do? she asked herself wildly. Even if Thornbury hadn't taken the cloak away, the letter she seeks is gone!

She jumped up then. She must go to the marquess at once and ask his advice, she decided as she struggled into a light pelisse and crammed a bonnet on her unruly curls. But stay! she thought as she searched for gloves and a reticule. He told me I was to go nowhere alone, so I must take a footman with me. But I can't do that! If I do, all the servants will know that I have been calling on an unmarried man. How ruinous that would be!

But I can't wait for a note to be delivered to him, she argued with herself, her soft lips setting in a firm line. It is almost noon. We do not have much time.

Convention be damned! I must go to him alone, she decided. And if that means disobeying his ridiculous order, so be it. He is not my guardian, after all.

She ran down the stairs and begged Tuttle to fetch her a hansom. "You do not take your maid, Miss Penelope?" he asked, eyeing her a little dubiously. "Or care to wait for the duke's carriage to be brought round?"

"There is no need for either," Penny said, with the sunniest smile she could muster. "I only go to Lady Manning's, and she will see me safely home."

The butler's wary look disappeared, and he smiled in relief. Penny suddenly felt the complete rogue.

As impatient as she was to see Thornbury, she did not quit the cab when it reached his house in Pall Mall until two elderly ladies who were walking by it were well past. Then, after looking quickly from left to right, she bounded out and ran up the steps, wishing her pelisse had a hood, so she could hide her hair and her features.

When he opened the door, Thornbury's butler was both astounded and suspicious, but Penny was desperate now. Pushing past him, so she was safely away from the stares of any passersby, she took a deep breath and said, "I am Miss Penelope Shaw. Please tell the marquess I call on a matter of great urgency. It is imperative that I see him at once."

When the butler just stared at her, she wanted to shake him. Suddenly a terrible thought invaded her mind, and she added, "He is *here*, is he not? Oh, please, you must tell me!"

"He is here, miss, but—"

"You are wasting my time!" Penny interrupted. "Go now and fetch him—or I shall start to scream!"

"There is no need for that, ma'am," a deep, bored voice said from somewhere above them. Penny looked up to see Thornbury coming leisurely down the stairs. He was dressed as impeccably as always. He in turn looked around the hall, and when he saw no maid with her, no strange footman, his face darkened with his displeasure.

Taking her arm in a tight grasp, he marched her to a salon nearby. "See that we are not disturbed!" he ordered over his shoulder just before he shut the door.

"Well!" he said before she could get a word out. "This is beyond anything, Miss Shaw! I did not think even *you* would be so bold! Are you determined to ruin your reputation in the most devastating way you can devise? And, I might add, mine as well? For if you are, you have certainly succeeded, and—"

"Oh, do be quiet!" Penny shouted. Stunned, he fell silent, and she rushed on, "We have no time for such silliness as reputations! I have had another note from Louisa Bellings, and I am frightened. She writes that if she does not get her cloak back by five this afternoon, she is going to do something bad to Phillipa or Uncle William, maybe even burn his house down! What am I to do? What *can* I do?"

"You brought that note with you?" he asked, holding out his hand.

Penny fumbled through her reticule. "It is here somewhere . . . I know I put it— Oh, here it is!"

The marquess read it quickly, his brows a solid bar across his forehead, he was frowning so. When he had finished, he dropped it on a table, then wiped his fingers on a handkerchief, as if merely touching such a thing had soiled them.

"Well?" Penny demanded in an awful voice. "Don't just stand there looking severe, sir! That will not serve! Tell me what I am to do!"

"*You* are to do nothing," he said coldly. "You may leave this matter in my hands."

"Well, I won't—and that's final," she said, crossing her arms before her and looking stubborn. "The very idea! And if you think to have me removed from your house bodily, I warn you I shall scream the neighborhood down. Then there'll be a disgrace you will never live down!"

"How fierce you are!" he said, a little smile twisting one corner of his mouth. Penny saw it and rushed to him, her fists upraised. He caught them easily in one big hand.

"No, you don't, wildcat!" he said as he maneuvered her backward until he could push her down on a chair. "That is quite enough! You will sit there and be quiet, pretending to be the lady you are not. If you behave yourself, I may—mind you, I *may*—tell you what I am going to do."

Penny glowered at him, her full lower lip outthrust, and it was all he could do not to bend and kiss it. Wondering where such an insane urge had come from, he waited until she nodded reluctantly.

He sat down himself then, across from her. "Fortunately, Sam Bottoms reported this morning that he had located the house where Louisa Bellings is staying."

"Bottoms is the man you have had looking for her?"

"Yes," he said, surprised she remembered. "Mrs. Bellings went to the tavern yesterday, and the owner pointed her out to him. It was a simple matter for him to follow her home. She is living with another demi—"

He paused and coughed then, and Penny said impatiently, "Stop being so Gothic! If you mean a demirep or a doxy or a dasher, say so and have done with it. I am not at all a prude."

"No, you're not, are you?" he agreed, looking stunned.

"Where is this house?" Penny demanded.

"That is not important for you to know. I intend to go there now and confront the woman. I shall tell her that her secret is out, and that the letter has been destroyed. And I shall insist she leave England entirely, unless she wants me to bring the law into this. I do not think I shall have much trouble with her. My only problem, Miss Shaw, is *you*. How the devil am I to get you out of here, sight unseen?"

"You have a back door? Mews behind the house? Nothing could be simpler. I'll just pop out that way, walk to the end of the mews, and hail a hackney."

"You'll do nothing of the sort!" Thornbury roared, looking harassed. "Are you insane? You wouldn't get as far as the corner before some groom accosted you. And there are other dangers. Who knows who might have followed you here? Louisa Bellings probably has at least one accomplice . . . in fact I am sure she does."

He saw Penny was considering this seriously, and he drew a shaky breath of relief.

"Perhaps I could just wait for you here then? I will be so glad to hear that Mrs. Bellings is vanquished. And later we could go for a drive, or something, and no one will think a thing of it."

"Obviously you have not spent much time studying yourself in the looking glass this morning," Thornbury said wryly. "But may I point out your pelisse is a blue check, your gown is a yellow-and-white floral pattern, and you are wearing beige house slippers. Furthermore, your bonnet is a violet trimmed with pink, and your reticule is green. You are a rainbow, Miss Shaw. And I have not even mentioned your hair. You have lost the ribbon again, and it is all undone. I don't think a drive can be considered. No, I must think of something else."

Penny blushed as she felt her hair and looked down at her attire. "Could I borrow your comb again, sir?" she asked meekly. "I am sure I can tidy it while you are gone."

"I'll have my butler bring you one, and anything else you need," he muttered. "Stay here. I'll try and be as quick as I can."

"Wait!" Penny called after him. As he turned, she said, "You will take a pistol, won't you? I mean, Mrs. Bellings may be dangerous, and I would feel just terrible if you were injured."

"Would you, brat?" he asked in a softer voice.

"I am not a brat! And of course I would feel guilty, since you are helping me and my family."

"That restores me to my proper place very neatly," he murmured as he opened the door. "Remember, on no account are you to leave this room!"

He was gone, the door closing behind him, before Penny could reply.

The marquess ordered his hat and gloves and driving coat, as well as his phaeton to be brought round at once. Then he gave instructions to his butler. That individual had regained his usual composure—and looked as if wild young ladies, dressed every which way, invaded the premises at least twice every week. Thornbury went into his study then and loaded two pistols, which he thrust into the deep pockets of his driving coat.

Only a few minutes passed before he was tooling the phaeton toward the address near Covent Garden that he had been given. His tiger, Perry, was seated beside him, listening carefully as Thornbury told him where they were going and for what reason. Perry knew the area. He had been born not far from Drury Lane, and had lived a precarious life on the streets until the marquess had rescued him. He often told himself there was nothing he would not do for his savior, and now his lips tightened as he realized he might have a chance to help him at last.

Thornbury left him in charge of the rig. It was getting a lot of attention in the street, but Perry ignored the stares and whispers as his master went up the steps and banged the knocker.

When Nan opened the door, her eyes widened. And when she tried to close it quickly, Thornbury was ready. He pushed it so hard that she staggered back and sat down abruptly on the first step of the flight of stairs.

"Louisa Bellings!" he called in a loud voice. "Louisa Bellings! You will come down at once, or I will come up and get you!"

He could hear two feminine voices arguing in loud whispers somewhere upstairs, and he waited, ignoring the frightened maid, who stared at him in horror.

"I said at once!" he called again.

There was silence for a moment, then a cool, amused voice said, "I shall be with you presently, sir. I am not dressed to receive callers. Nan, show the gentleman to the parlor and bring him some wine."

"I prefer to await you here, ma'am," Thornbury told his unseen adversary. "And I wouldn't touch any wine in this house."

It was several minutes later before the woman he

198

knew must be Louisa Bellings came slowly down the stairs. She was dressed in a simple morning gown a duchess would not have scorned, with her raven hair arranged simply. She wore nothing more on her lovely face than a winsome smile, and altogether she looked the complete lady. She paused when she reached the bottom step to stare down at the terrified maid who crouched there.

"She may go," Thornbury said. Nan was quick to scurry away.

"Won't you come into the parlor now, sir?" Mrs. Bellings invited as she curtsied. Thornbury did not bow in return, but he followed her meekly enough.

He left the door open and waited for her to be seated before he took his own seat—where he could see not only her, but also the hall beyond.

"You are Thornbury, of course," Mrs. Bellings said, smiling still.

Her soft tones were so unlike the vicious note she had sent to Penny Shaw that he had to admit she was a most accomplished actress.

"So, you know my name."

She looked down at the hands she had clasped in her lap. His voice had been hard, scornful, but she did not show resentment.

Raising her eyes to his again, she fluttered her lashes. "Yes, I do. Mr. Pettibone told me of you several times. And, of course, I have often seen you this Season in the company of a young friend of mine, Penny Shaw."

"You are no friend of Miss Shaw's, ma'am. Far from it. But enough of this sparring. I am here as the girl's emissary."

"Indeed? She has told you of my cloak? I would never have thought a duke's niece would stoop to theft, but people have strange compulsions sometimes, do they not? You may tell Miss Shaw I shall say nothing more of the matter after my cloak is returned to me. I am not a vindictive woman, and I mean her no harm."

Thornbury's laugh was not a pleasant sound. "No, you only mean to harm her sister and her uncle. Of course, if she were in the duke's house when it caught fire, she might well perish, too."

Louisa Bellings stared at him, her eyes narrowing. So, he knew all about it, did he? Damn the girl!

"I was growing weary of writing to her, and only thought to frighten her," she said. "Of course I had no intention of harming anyone. But I must have my cloak back."

"Unfortunately, that is impossible. It has been destroyed."

"Destroyed?" she whispered through a suddenly dry throat. "How came that to happen?"

"I ordered it done. After, of course, I discovered the secret pocket sewn to the lining—and read the letter that pocket contained."

Mrs. Bellings stared at him in horror, and he went on, "I myself personally burned that letter. So you see, there is no need for you to fret about your cloak anymore."

He watched her face change from sweet demureness to an ice-cold mask of hatred, and he braced himself. When she reached into her pocket and drew out a pistol, he was ready. He jumped up and grasped her wrist, tightening that grasp until the pistol fell to the floor. Louisa Bellings attacked him then, kicking and scratching him, and all the while swearing at him in a loud, vicious voice. Thornbury had never struck a woman in his life, but he had no choice here. He slapped her with an open palm and tried to soften his swing, but still her head whipped to one side, and she cried out.

Kicking the pistol to the far side of the room, he forced her to sit down again. As he backed away, he drew one of his own pistols from his pocket and aimed it at her.

She was crying now, both hands to her face. Crying and moaning in her frustration and disappointment. Thornbury waited quietly until her sobs died away and she raised her head to stare at him. When she saw the pistol he held, she shrank back in her chair.

"An edifying display," he said. "Alastair always had the most deplorable taste! Just as well he has left the country.

"As you, Mrs. Bellings—if that's who you are—are about to do, too. I really do not think either Miss Shaw or I would have a moment's comfort if you were still free here."

"And if I refuse to go?" she asked, desperately trying to get control of the situation.

"You will not be so stupid. You see, if you are not gone in twenty-four hours, I will be forced to take this matter further. To the law, and to that government figure you thought to blackmail. And since royalty is also involved, I am sure you can see your continued residence here would be most unwise. The Tower is so unpleasant!"

He waited patiently while she thought about it. At last she shrugged. "I see I have no choice," she said in a bitter voice. "But I have little money. Surely you would not cast me adrift penniless, m'lord!"

"I assure you I would," came the relentless reply.

Louisa Bellings looked stunned.

"What do you intend to tell your accomplice?" he asked next. "Surely he will be disappointed, too, that your scheme did not work."

"I have no intention of telling him anything," she muttered. "Tear me limb from limb, he would, if he knew. No, I must leave England, and I must do so at once."

"A wise decision, ma'am. There is a ship sailing with the tide tonight for the Bahamas. I suggest you procure passage on it. And I might even be tempted to help you with your fare, if you will give me your accomplice's name. You see, if you go away, leaving him in the dark, there's no saying that he wouldn't continue his pursuit of Miss Shaw. So in exchange for your passage to a new life, I shall require a letter to him that can be posted after you sail, and his name as well."

She looked stubborn for only a moment, then she shrugged again. "I've no idea what his real first name is. He has always been called Blackie in the rookery. Blackie Gorton. Yes, I'll write the letter."

When she handed the letter to Thornbury a few minutes later, he pocketed it and gave her a purse of guineas in exchange.

They had not spoken for some time, but after picking her pistol up to take with him and going to the door, the marquess said, "Tonight, Mrs. Bellings. If you are still here tomorrow, I'll notify the law. Or perhaps I will just tell this Blackie?"

Louisa stared at the empty doorway, not even hearing the front door close behind him. She was still staring when April crept down the stairs, her china blue eyes wide.

But when she would have questioned her, Louisa waved an impatient hand. "I've no time to waste!" she said curtly. "Get Nan. Tell her she must go to the docks and get me a place on the ship that is sailing to the Bahamas tonight. I'll also need a carter later, for my trunk."

She smiled then. "You've been good to me, April, and I won't forget that. In fact, so you won't get in trouble, I'll leave here now—go somewhere else till dark."

"Maybe that would be best," April said, looking relieved.

202

She was a little surprised when Louisa gave her a hearty kiss, for she was not a woman given to loving gestures.

"And because I'm so fond of you, I'll do you another favor and take that canary off your hands," Louisa said, smiling broadly now.

"But what will I tell m'lord when he returns and it's gone?"

"Tell him it died, and you threw the cage away because you couldn't bear to be reminded of its loss. You know the form."

April grinned back at her, then thanked her. A short time later, Louisa Bellings left the house carrying a small portmanteau and the canary in its cage. She hailed a hansom cab and had the driver take her to a goldsmith's shop she knew. At the door, she released the canary. It seemed confused for a moment, then it flew away.

Louisa made a very good bargain for the cage. Sometime before she had noticed it was made of almost pure gold. She remembered thinking April's m'lord must be besotted indeed to give her such a lavish gift, and she grinned when she pictured his reaction when April told him she had thrown the cage away.

Poor April, she thought with a sly smile as she climbed into the cab again. Doesn't have the brains God gave a flea! But thank heavens I do!

Fifteen

THORNBURY WAS NOT absent for very long, but to Penny Shaw the time he was gone seemed endless. For a while, after she had tidied her hair, she amused herself investigating the salon where she had been left, but that activity soon palled. She thought it a stiff room, and although it was richly decorated and filled with lovely furniture, somehow it seemed too cold and formal to be comfortable. There were no books or journals to read, and not even a carelessly discarded pair of gloves or a riding crop marred the shining surfaces of the tables. There was nothing much to see out the windows, either. The room faced a narrow side yard and the marble walls of the mansion next door.

It needs flowers, Penny thought, and a little disorder. Even an open workbasket or a needlepoint frame set in the window would help. She shook her head then, for such things were a woman's belongings, and the marquess was not married. She wondered why he was not. He must be in his late twenties now. Wasn't he concerned about his heir? She had thought all the nobility were.

Finally she sat down where she could see the mantel clock. The hands had never moved so slowly, and she began to wonder if anything had gone wrong. She was considering a number of dire possibilities in her mind when she heard Thornbury's voice in the hall at last. Relieved he had not been shot from ambush, or taken prisoner by a gang of Louisa Bellings's toughs, Penny ran to him as he entered—and quite without thinking of what she was doing, hugged him to her tightly.

Startled, the marquess put his own arms around her, staring down at the top of her fiery head, which was all he could see since she had buried her face in his cravat. To its detriment, he was sure, but somehow he did not care as his hands caressed her back.

Suddenly she drew back, and he let her go.

"I—I do beg your pardon, sir!" she said. Her face was so hot she knew it must be crimson. "I have no idea why I did that! But I have been so worried! It has taken you so long!"

"Less than an hour. There was no need for any concern. Everything went smoothly. Louisa Bellings is vanquished and sails for the Bahamas tonight. And I have the name of her accomplice," he said slowly and calmly, to give her time to recover.

"Who is he?" Penny demanded.

Well, it didn't take her long, he thought ruefully. I might have known. Aloud, he said, "I suppose it can do no harm to tell you. Even *you* will be hardly likely to run into him after tomorrow. His name is Blackie Gorton, and he operates in one of London's most unsavory neighborhoods. Mrs. Bellings was persuaded to write him a letter, telling him the game was up."

Penny beamed at him. "So, it does end well, then! I am so glad."

"It is not quite ended yet, Miss Shaw," Thornbury said, looking grim. "There remains one problem, and a formidable one it is, too."

He paused, and Penny considered for a moment. Then she said in a little voice, "Oh. You mean me."

"I do, indeed. Somehow I must spirit you out of this house and return you to the duke's with no one the wiser. If you have any idea how that might be accomplished, I beg you to enlighten me. I must admit I am fresh out of possibilities."

"Come now, sir! There are endless things we might do," she said in rallying tones. "For one, I could dress as a boy, perhaps a boot boy, or even one of your maids, and—"

"Not with that hair blazing like a torch, you can't."

"Oh. Well, I suppose if you were to write to the duke and tell him I am here, he could come and get me. No one would think a thing of it, if I left in his company.

"Still, I wish we could think of another way. Uncle William was so angry at Deirdre this morning for not telling him that George had almost been kidnapped, I'd as lief not anger him again—not when he has suggested I live with him from now on, and not in Northumberland with my aunt Eliza."

"Yes, I can see that keeping in his good graces would be a powerful incentive for you. At least until you do the next impossible thing."

Penny ignored the insult. "Well, we could simply wait until dark, and then take a chance on escaping notice."

"I do not think it at all a good idea to have you here for that length of time," Thornbury told her, his voice frosty.

Penny swallowed, but she put up her chin as well. "I do not think it is very helpful, m'lord, for you to do nothing but ridicule my suggestions!" she said firmly. "But if you want my honest opinion, I think we should just go to the stables and drive off in your phaeton. Unless someone should see us coming out of the mews, where's the harm? And I've often found that sometimes the simplest solution is the best one, if you are brave enough to carry it off. Chances are we will escape notice entirely."

"Are you sure you do not mean 'brazen,' rather

than 'brave'?" he asked. Then he threw out his hands. "Very well, Miss Shaw. It shall be as you say. I told Perry to keep the phaeton ready, on the odd chance I would need it again. While you don that unsuitable bonnet and pelisse again, I'll just send a message to him. And let us hope we come out of this with a whole skin. Both of us," he added grimly as he went to the door.

If Thornbury's tiger was astounded to see Miss Shaw accompanying his master and being helped to her seat in the phaeton by him, he showed no sign of it. And his expression remained wooden even when the marquess ordered him to the end of the mews, telling him to signal only when there were no smart carriages coming in either direction.

"Queer do, this," Perry muttered as he set off. "I wonder what the guv is doin' with that strange-looking bird. Never seed such an outfit in all my days!"

When the signal came at last, Thornbury drove quickly down the mews, Penny hiding her face in a handkerchief as she had been instructed. He slowed only so Perry could jump up behind, before he headed toward Berkeley Square.

"I do believe we've done it!" he said more cheerfully. "You may put that handkerchief away, Miss Shaw."

As Penny tucked it back in her reticule, she smiled at him. "You see?" she crowed. "Simplicity, m'lord. Simplicity—"

"Beggin' yer pardon, milord," Perry interrupted. "I think we're bein' followed."

Penny would have turned to look, except Thornbury said harshly, "Face front! Whoever it is must not know we suspect anything. But to make sure you're right, Perry, I'll try a few aimless turns."

"Who could it be?" Penny asked him as he took the first one.

"Whoever followed you to my house this morning, I imagine," he said. "He must have been watching you. Waiting for his chance."

He turned into yet another street, and said in a louder voice, "Is he still behind us, Perry?"

"Aye, that he is."

"Do you know who it is?"

"Never seed him afore, milord. Driving a gig, he is—and he's a big 'un. Black hair and beard, and some fierce-looking!"

Penny stole a glance at Thornbury's face and saw how rigid it had become.

"He's got a bang-up pair, too," Perry continued. Penny did not know how Thornbury's face could get any grimmer, but somehow it did.

"All right. Say no more. I must think," he said as he turned into Piccadilly.

Penny wondered if he was planning on trying to lose the man in Hyde Park, but he drove straight on to Knightsbridge. As they got farther and farther from the center of town, he urged his team to a canter. Penny thought escape this way most unwise. Surely they were safer surrounded by crowds, and other vehicles!

"Where are we going?" she asked at last, clutching her bonnet lest she lose it in the breeze of their passage.

"Still trailing us, Perry?"

"Aye, but not gainin'. Don't drive to an inch by no means."

"That's good. Now, Miss Shaw, I'm hoping for a miracle—and if you have an ounce of sense, you'll be praying for one as well," he told her.

"You think that's Blackie, don't you?" she asked next.

His nod was curt, for all his attention was on his team. A short time later, he turned in between a pair of imposing gates and drove swiftly up a winding drive. The phaeton's wheels crunched on the gravel, and when he halted the team out of sight of the highroad, they all held their breaths and listened. There was no sign of pursuit.

"Well, that was a successful ploy, at any rate," Thornbury said more easily. "I knew he would not dare enter here."

"Where are we?" Penny asked.

"These are the gardens of Mr. Joshua Biggs. They are not open to the public, but Mr. Biggs is always delighted when the nobility comes to admire his work. Today, however, I do not think we will do that. I must try and see if there is another way out."

He drove on again until they reached an open space. There were two other carriages there, one of them containing a man who must have just arrived, and Thornbury smiled for the first time in some hours.

"Whitaker!" he said as the phaeton came to a halt. "Well met, old chap, well met!"

Bartholomew Whitaker took in Penny's appearance without the blink of an eye as he bowed slightly.

"Something amiss, Thornbury?" he asked. "You sound less than your usual composed self, indeed you do."

"How can you doubt it, when you see I have Miss Shaw beside me?" Thornbury asked. Silently Penny seethed. "But I cannot explain it now. There is no time.

"Whitaker, I must ask an enormous favor of you. It involves Miss Shaw's safety."

"You need say no more," Whitaker told him. "I am, as always, completely at your service, Miss Shaw."

Penny gave him her glowing smile, and he smiled in return.

"If you two will stop doing the pretty, we can begin," Thornbury growled, his voice cold again. Penny turned to stare at him.

"I want to change rigs with you, Bart," he said. "And coats as well. How fortunate we are both dark and about the same size! Then I want you to take my tiger up beside you."

He turned to Penny then and began to untie the ribbons of her bonnet. "What on earth are you doing?" she asked, catching hold of his hands

"Insuring your old age, ma'am. There," he added as he drew the bonnet from her curls. "Remove your pelisse as well."

Penny opened her mouth to protest, but one look at his stern face told her that if she did not obey him, and at once, he was quite capable of stripping it from her himself.

"Now, Perry," he said, turning to a tiger who was beginning to look quite apprehensive, "you are to pretend you are Miss Shaw. Don these things and pull the bonnet well down over your ears. Maybe the fact your hair is short and ash brown to boot will be less noticeable that way. And I think if you would cling to Whitaker's arm, and turn your face into his sleeve, as if overcome with fright or some-such, it might just be convincing."

Penny only dared a quick glimpse at Perry, lest she laugh, for his face was so horrified. "Dress up as a *wench*? No, no," he croaked. "Milord, don't ask it o' me!"

"I would not do so, if it were not entirely necessary. But I am too large to pretend to be Miss Shaw. Otherwise, I assure you I would do it, for her life may be in danger."

As he had spoken, he had been removing his coat, taking the one Whitaker handed him. After he had shrugged into it, he handed the reins to Penny and jumped down. Penny could hear Perry mumbling under his breath behind her, and nobly, she did not turn around.

"Do you have a rug, Bart?" Thornbury asked. "I'll need something to cover Miss Shaw with, since she must crouch on the floorboards of the carriage."

"What?" Penny asked as she climbed down to stand beside the two men.

"Listen, and listen well!" the marquess said. "Blackie, or whoever it was, saw us drive in here. A man, a girl, and a groom. He did not see Mr. Whitaker arrive, and he, fortunately, is alone. We will leave here first in his carriage and behind his roans. All Blackie will see is a solitary gentleman in a blue coat instead of a gray one. He will not follow us. No, he will wait for my rig to leave the grounds."

"But won't he wonder where your tiger has gone when we leave?" Whitaker asked.

"We must hope he will have forgotten him in the excitement of the chase." He paused for a moment, then added, "I don't think he'll try anything if you take him by surprise. Wait quite a while before you leave. Delay might make him grow careless. Then turn south, away from London, and drive like hell. Here, you'd better have one of my pistols, just in case."

"You do understand, Thornbury, that I do this for Miss Shaw alone," Whitaker said. "And as payment, I shall expect a complete explanation from the two of you as soon as the adventure is over."

"And you shall have it, and gladly!" the marquess said, with a warm smile, as the two men shook hands. "Time we were off. Perry, where are you?"

His servant did not answer or come out from behind the phaeton, where he had concealed himself. It was true he had said he would do anything for the master, but he had never thought it would come to something like this! And what if one of his mates should see him? He'd never live it down!

211

"Perry, come out now!" The order came again, and he took a deep breath and sidled around the wheel.

Penny controlled herself with great effort, noticing that neither of the two men seemed to be having any trouble at all looking solemn. But when she saw Perry was mortified, all her sympathy was aroused, and she lost the urge to laugh.

"Yes, you are very convincing," Thornbury told him. "Just push the bonnet back a bit. It is not worn so, half covering the face."

"I must thank you for doing this," Penny said as she came and took the tiger's hands in hers. "I think you must be very brave, to make such a sacrifice so I can be safe. I shall never forget it."

"Nor I, my boy," Thornbury said as he gave Perry a rough hug. The tiger suddenly looked easier.

"You may discard the costume as soon as Mr. Whitaker feels it is safe. My thanks to you, too, Bart. And never fear—you shall have a most *detailed* explanation.

"Now, Miss Shaw, if you would just climb into Whitaker's rig and scrunch down. Try to make yourself as small as you can. You can hang on to my boots for balance. Yes, that is very well."

He got into the phaeton himself then and covered his legs and Penny Shaw with the carriage rug. "I shall not ask if you are comfortable, ma'am, for I am sure you are not."

"It is quite all right, sir," the carriage rug said as her two arms wrapped around his shining boots.

Thornbury drove down the drive at a sedate pace, but even so Penny was bounced about a little, and she was not looking forward to the highroad at all. Full of ruts and holes, it was nowhere near as well kept as this drive. She pulled herself up a little to brace her back against the seat.

"Sit still!" came the order from above her. "We are almost to the gates."

Penny swayed a little as he took the corner, and she held her breath and prayed. The rig turned toward London, still being driven at a sedate pace, and she heard no shouts or sounds of pursuit. After what seemed an age, she hissed, "Why are we going so slowly? Surely it would be better to get away as quickly as possible!"

"No, it would not! We must do nothing to arouse his suspicions. I think the deception worked, however. He was some little distance from the gates and could not see me clearly. And he gave me only a cursory glance. The roans, of course, convinced him, that and the fact he thinks I am alone."

"When can I come out?" Penny asked, bouncing on the hard floorboards and wincing as one of the wheels went into a hole.

"Not for a while yet," came the implacable reply. "I want to be sure he will not change his mind and decide to investigate more closely. Indeed, it might be better if you remained where you are until I have you safe at your uncle's house. Remember, you don't even have an unsuitable bonnet or pelisse now."

"I absolutely refuse to suffocate in here for that distance!" the carriage rug exclaimed, and Thornbury smiled grimly to himself. "Convention be hanged!"

"What a truly inappropriate thing for a young lady to say," he remarked through gritted teeth. It was strange. Only minutes before he had been frantic to get her safely away, but now that he was sure they had escaped Blackie Gorton, he found he was losing his temper rapidly. Miss Penny Shaw was about to have a most needed lesson taught to her, and he was delighted he was to be the one to administer it.

"Uncle William said it this morning, and if he can, so can I!" Penny's muffled, indignant voice said.

"He is a man, not a young chit of a thing who is not even out."

"May I remind you, *you* have nothing to say about any expressions I might use, m'lord!"

When there was no reply to this provocative remark, Penny fell silent. She was already getting sore from the jouncing she was receiving, and she was reminded of her trip to London on the load of firewood. The marquess wasn't going much faster than the farmer had, either. She wished he would do so.

As if Thornbury had read her thoughts, he dropped his hands; the roans broke into a canter. Penny gasped and moaned as, over and over, her bottom rose and then slapped down hard on the bare wood floorboards. I will not ask if I can sit beside him again, no matter how much it hurts! she vowed. I won't give him the satisfaction of making me beg!

After what seemed an eternity, Laurence Russell was forced to slow the team as they reached London traffic again. Penny swallowed a relieved sigh, lest he hear it.

"Very well, Miss Shaw. There is no one near at the moment. You may come out now, but be quick about it," he said from above her.

Still clutching one of his boots for balance, Penny inched to the other side of the phaeton, stifling her groans. Pushing the rug aside, she scrambled to the padded seat.

She knew she must look a perfect fright, for her hair was streaming down her back again, and stray curls whipped across her cheeks. She reached up to smooth them, even though she knew how futile a gesture that was.

When she glanced at the marquess, her eyes were stony. "You did that deliberately, didn't you?" she asked, her voice enraged.

"Did what?" came the bland reply.

"Picked up the pace like that, so I would suffer.

And since Blackie never followed us at all, there was no need for me to have to hide under the rug all this time, either. It was just spite and vindictiveness, and I think you are horrid!"

He did not reply or turn to her as he weaved through the press of vehicles, heading for Berkeley Square. Penny thought she saw a fleeting satisfied smile cross his face, and she was furious.

"Perhaps I did it to punish you," he said as they entered Charles Street. "Because, Miss Shaw, this entire misadventure was most unnecessary. You had only to be prudent and follow my order not to go anywhere alone. Then after receiving Louisa Bellings's letter, and mine tonight, this Blackie Gorton would have never come near you. But you were not obedient, or very wise, were you? No, not *you*! *You* had to rush to my house, and unattended, too, I remind you, putting a great many people at risk. If Whitaker or my tiger come to any harm from your smug righteousness that *you* always know best, I'll see you are sorry for it!

"I shall say nothing of the brazen way you have been flirting with Whitaker ever since Countess Hasting's musicale—yes, I was told about your long, private tête-à-tête with him—for it pales beside today's debacle."

Penny's mouth had fallen open halfway through this tirade. How dare he take me to task! she thought. She had only been trying to protect her sister and her uncle! And who was he to chastise her for flirting? Not that she had, she reminded herself.

"You are the most impossible, arrogant, *overbearing* man!" she gasped.

"And you are the most irritating, irresponsible, *sorry* excuse for a young lady that I have ever had the misfortune to know!" he snapped as he halted the team before Duke Longford's house.

So furious were they both, so totally immersed in

215

their quarrel, they did not notice the attention they were receiving. The park in the center of the square was crowded this lovely afternoon. Gunter's was enjoying a brisk patronage as well. Several people pointed to the wild-haired young lady in the smart phaeton—and her angry, stern-faced driver—and whispered among themselves.

"Well!" Penny said, indignant anew. "I cannot tell you, then, how happy I am this whole affair is over, and I never have to see you again! And furthermore—"

But what she had been about to say was never uttered, for Thornbury had tied the reins to the post at the front of the carriage used for that purpose and put both his large hands around her slender throat.

"Be quiet!" he growled, leaning closer. "It would take so little effort to throttle you, Miss Shaw, thus sparing the world any more of your catastrophes. I must admit I am sorely tempted."

For a second his fingers tightened, and Penny felt a tremor of alarm. But no, she told herself, he would not dare. Not here, not now. She stared up into his face, only inches from her own, and her lips parted in surprise as his expression softened and a light came into his eyes that she had never seen there before. And as he remained close to her, so very close, she felt as if her insides were melting as fast as one of Gunter's ices.

"I must be insane!" he muttered, shaking his head as if to clear it. "Completely, totally, utterly . . ."

He bent closer to kiss her. Penny told herself she did not dare try to evade that kiss while he still had her throat between his hands. But after only a moment, she knew that for the lie it was. How lovely his mouth felt on hers! she thought, bewildered. How warm and insistent, how passionate and gentle at the same time! Why, she had never dreamed kissing could be this nice! And when

Laurence Russell let go of her throat at last, to catch her tight in his arms, she only put her own arms around him in complete surrender.

". . . insane!" he murmured, finally finishing his sentence as he raised his mouth an inch from hers.

"Why—why did you do that?" Penny asked, regretting the ending of his kiss more than she had ever regretted anything in her life.

He smiled down at her, and her eyes widened. "I have wanted to for some time. Especially this morning when you ran to me and hugged me. You say I think of you as a child, but that isn't so, Penny. You are a lovely young woman, and I want you to be mine. And the reason I chastised you for flirting with Whitaker was because I was so jealous of him. It is all clear to me now. Besides, why do you think I embroiled myself in your problems? Because I enjoy strife and danger and unconventionality? Of course not!"

"I won't marry you," Penny said, her heart racing. "I won't! You would make my life miserable."

"Then we are well-matched indeed, for you are certain to make mine miserable, too," he said, his deep voice only a little unsteady. "But I am sure there will be other times when we will find ourselves in . . . um . . . complete accord. Like just now when I kissed you."

"But there is more to marriage than kissing!" Penny protested weakly.

As he drew back, he smiled, cocking one brow at her, and Penny felt the heat rise in her cheeks. As she hid her face in his cravat and clutched his lapels, he said, "I cannot tell you how much I am looking forward to exploring all of it with you. Even looking forward to sharing a comb with you over the years," he added as he smoothed her hair back. A curl wound itself around his finger, capturing it.

At the library window above them, William

217

Shaw, Duke Longford, smiled to himself and nodded in satisfaction. And Phillipa Shaw gasped while Christopher Blakely chuckled where they stood at a drawing room window on the first floor, arms around each other.

Only Lady Eliza Shaw missed the excitement. From her bedroom window, she had been the first to see her difficult niece coming home in the Marquess of Thornbury's company. And when she saw how untidy the girl was, how wanton she looked without even a bonnet on those flaming curls, she had fainted with the shock.

The couple in the phaeton seemed completely oblivious to any interested spectators, however, as they continued to gaze deeply into each other's eyes.

"Tiresome brat!" Thornbury murmured, his hands cupping her face, his tender smile giving the lie to the name he called her.

"Arrogant know-all!" she replied unsteadily, smiling mistily at him in return.

One of the duke's footmen arrived to take charge of the team then, and Thornbury seemed to notice for the first time that they were not alone.

As he lifted Penny from the carriage, he said, "Now see what you have made me do! I won't have a shred of reputation left with the ton after today."

Penny considered him for a moment, head tipped to one side. Then she beckoned him closer and said, "The ton be hanged, sir—and convention, too!"

And in perfect accord for the very first time, they entered the house, laughing together.

'Maybe you should talk to someone too,' I persisted. 'You often seem very upset, agitated.'

'I am upset,' she said. 'Which is why I need *you* to talk to Martin.' I couldn't resist Susan.

I talked to him a few weeks later, when we were drying ourselves off after showering after a game of touch. He still had the most fantastic body. He was big and strong and had an impressive grace about him.

'Susan thinks you're depressed.'

'Low level misery—flashes of—curse of the Irish.'

'She thinks it's more. I think you need to take this seriously. Talk about it. Think about it. Get Susan to help you.'

'Susan? Help me? You're kidding!' He turned to me. 'Phil, you're my oldest and dearest friend but Susan's put you up to this. Ask her why she doesn't talk to me about my depression or whatever she chooses to call my psychic state. Ask her why we need you as a go between.'

'Well, that might be the problem.'

'Shit Phil. Fucking grow up.' He was angry, slight menacing. 'You're her friend, not mine. You don't give a shit about me or what you call my depression, so don't pretend you do.' He flicked me with his towel, hard enough to hurt. 'Have some fucking integrity. If you want to play spiritual counsellor do it with us both there.' He walked out, but the next time we met it was as if it had never happened. Martin wasn't one to hold grudges.

I wanted to revive my friendship with him but he was right that we had ceased being close friends quite a long time ago. There wasn't the intimacy we had once had.

'I do care about you, Martin,' I said.

'Sure thing,' he said. 'Next you'll be hugging me.'

'He won't listen,' I told Susan. 'I don't think he understands what is happening to him. Or wants to.'

I remained her confidante, guilty as sin.

Martin

I tried to be happy with Susan. After breaking off the relationship with Melissa and then the incident with Yvette, I tried. My unhappiness seemed shameful, to exhibit it even more so. I gritted my teeth, tried to grin and bear it.

The worst was the loneliness, going home at night. It stopped feeling like home.

'Oh hello, Martin.' It felt as genuine as the welcome in a four-star hotel. 'Ben crashed into bed at six. He had swimming this afternoon. Then Joshie and I ate dinner. We got hungry, didn't we Joshie?'

It hurt. The kids were lined up against me. I was the bruiser who was late to dinner. I was the one who was too rough in games. I wasn't such a good parent, but I wasn't as bad as they thought. I could see it in Joshie's eyes. Here he comes. All the peace and calm with Mummy will go down the tube. He'd do anything to resist me—grizzle, cry, hurt his arm, be polite or ineffectually cooperative. I could see him caught between us, the ideological battle between good and evil. Sometimes I hated him for how easily he capitulated to her, but I could remember being the child who had stood between his parents. I tried to keep the door open to the kids. Occasionally the Irish in me slammed it shut.

'There's some bread and cheese in the kitchen,' she'd say, 'and the cold lamb kebabs from Sunday. I'm putting Joshie to bed and then I'm going myself.'

Later I'd go in, and she'd be asleep, her small body resolutely defining her side of the bed. I'd reach out to her, out of desperation, and very occasionally she would allow me to make love to her. It was an allowance, a small one at that. It seemed to fuel my resentment against her, rather than pacify it. I wanted to love her. I did love her and it felt as if she was going out of her way to deny my love.

I got into the habit of putting off the loneliness, stopping at the Coogee Bay Hotel for a drink on the way home from work. Lots of faces I knew from my days doing criminal trials, lots of hard faces, lots of talk, lots of violence some nights. It was human emotion, human activity, human warmth and laughter. I'd sit there and watch, sipping my beer, gathering some sort of grim comfort, then steel myself to go home.

It was outside the hotel that the accident happened. I still can't put together quite what happened. Melissa was in my head. Warm, brown, loving Melissa. Melissa, Melissa. It was a year since I'd seen her. She was in my head most of the time.

But having a woman in your head when you're driving doesn't cause an accident. It was drizzling rain in the summer heat, the water steaming off the road as soon as it hit. Round eight. Daylight saving, the sun just about to go down, light bouncing off the wet.

He ran out on the road. I hit the brakes too late and he was on the windscreen, his face distorted against the glass. Red T-shirt. A thud as he hit the road and bounced hard against it. Two youths banging on my windscreen calling me 'cunt'.

I was out of the car. One of them tried to punch me. The kid in the red T-shirt, late teens, looked bad lying there on the road, blood coming out of his mouth and ear. I was shaking like a leaf. There was the sound of sirens coming closer, then the ambos and the cops were there. Another bloke was standing there, wearing a white apron, from the hot dog stand. 'It wasn't your fault. He ran out.' Then he disappeared. Down at the cop shop I answered questions. Polite and respectful but the cops had an edge of triumph having a solicitor in custody with two witnesses swearing I was going too fast, hadn't stopped in time, guilty as sin.

Me thinking, the kid's probably dead. Someone's son. The image in my head, his face smashed against my windscreen.

I rang Susan. No, she couldn't come down and collect me. The children were asleep. Five minutes away. She couldn't come. Her voice was cold. Bitch.

They found the hot dog man. The other blokes had chased the red T-shirt kid out onto the road. Part of a punch up. Someone else saw it too. I wasn't guilty but I'd hurt the kid. Or killed him. The cops couldn't say. He was still in intensive care.

I walked home in the rain, the boy's broken face in my head.

'I'm sorry I couldn't come,' she said. 'The children.'

'I ran into someone,' I said. 'I needed you there.'

'But it wasn't your fault.'

'Don't you understand? What it might feel like? That I might have liked you there?'

'I'm sorry,' she said, with a trace of guilt. 'The children . . . Martin . . . it wasn't your fault.'

'Oh good,' I said. 'Every time I get a picture of him in my head, his face smashed against the windscreen, I'll just remind myself it wasn't my fault. Bloody hell! That helps. Sorry, I hadn't thought of it. I just thought about some kid smashed against my car. But shit, look on the bright side. Insurance might even pay for the windscreen.'

'Martin, please . . .'